# The Tiger who Sleeps Under My Chair

Hannah Foley grew up in Devon, surrounded by green fields and spare tractor parts. She worked as an illustrator and designer in Scotland, before returning to Devon where she now lives with her three children. She works as a specialist nurse for people with multiple sclerosis and spends her spare time writing, drawing and digging on her allotment.

# The Tiger who Sleeps Under My Chair

## HANNAH FOLEY

ZEPHYR

An imprint of Head of Zeus

Head of Zeus Ltd
5–8 Hardwick Street
London EC1R 4RG

WWW.HEADOFZEUS.COM

*For Rich, who knows*

'There is more to us than some of us suppose'

Wendell Berry

*London, September 1884*

Emma took a deep breath and slid out from the shadows. She fumbled for her ammonite fossil. Under normal circumstances, she left the attic once a year and never alone. In the last half an hour, she'd crept down the narrow staircase three times, only to dart back again, tears of desperation welling in her eyes. If her father or Mrs Carter should catch her now...

She squeezed the fossil. The ancient spiral shell reassured her. This time she was not giving up.

It was the sight of the letter, which made Emma break the rules. She'd seen her name, written in James's bounding scrawl, tucked in a bundle under Tilly's arm when the housemaid came to collect her tray.

I

The morning's post was destined for Father's study, as always when he was home. Tilly would never dare disobey Mr Linden by not delivering it. The difficulty was, Emma's father had kept letters from her before. Perhaps he feared the contents would overexcite her, but James dismissed that – nothing exciting ever happened at his dismal boarding school.

Emma tiptoed along the corridor. Charles Linden was not violent – Emma had never heard her father raise his voice – but he ruled their London townhouse with icy control. He was as unfeeling as a locked door, as unyielding as a bank vault.

But she *must* read this letter. Their summer had ended so oddly with the stoat caught in the trap and that man with the gun. She and Olivier had been shocked, but James's reaction... She'd felt anxious ever since, waiting for news from her brother. She couldn't bear that her father might keep it from her.

Emma was grateful for the thick carpet runners and heavy draped fabrics, which soaked up sound like litmus paper sucking up water. But the fear that made Emma linger wasn't only the fear of being caught.

'*Solitude, silence, rational thought.*' She repeated the doctors' orders under her breath. These were the measures that kept her fragile health intact. Father would be horrified to know of the churning of her gut. Emma was horrified herself. It was stronger than any logic.

She crept downstairs to the first floor, barely daring to breathe. The door to her father's study stood open. The science which explained how her fossil had been made, also explained how gravity worked, how her breath made steam on a cold day. The universe was governed by scientific laws, stable and sure.

She paused in the doorway, ready to fly at the slightest sound.

The room was small, poorly lit by a narrow window, and made darker still by the uniform green binding of her father's books. The morning's post was stacked neatly in the centre of his desk.

Memories crowded in upon her. She remembered gazing up at her father, not understanding why he was so angry.

'Stand up straight, Emma. Pay attention. I am speaking of madness.'

She'd struggled to grasp most of what he'd said, though the words were etched in her mind.

'Madness, Emma! It took every effort of the doctors to bring you back to yourself. This fit is possibly the same mental weakness that possessed your mother. I will not lose you to it as well. You must dedicate yourself to cool logic and calm reason. It is your only hope. *My* only hope. These will be your defences against the tide of emotional instability. Solitude, silence, rational thought. And seclusion. With the exception of Kersbrook, you are not to leave the attic.'

Emma gripped the cold, hard edge of the desk, the room spinning. Was she going to have a fit? But she *must* read James's letter and hear from him in his own words.

She snatched up the post and carefully opened the flap on the envelope, hoping her father would think it had come un-gummed by itself.

 *St Scabrous School, Bournemouth, Sept 1884*

*Dearest Emma,*
*   It's hard to be back at school. Back to cold showers, bullying prefects and stiff collars. Didn't we have a summer, Em? The best yet*

*and all the better for Olivier coming too. I
shall remember it for ever.*

*Do you dream of Devon, Em, now that you
are in London?*

*I do. I dream of Kersbrook almost every
night. It is perfect and every house should
be made in its image. I dream of the fishing
boats pulled up on the pebbles under the red
cliffs and how we bought mackerel from the
fishermen. I can smell them as Dillis cooks
them for supper. Remember how Father turned
his nose up? Far too fishy for him!*

*Even when I'm awake, I find myself
dreaming of Kersbrook. The sea sparkling
in the sunshine and the coolness of the water
as I dive in from the boat. You'll think me
ridiculous, but on my first night, I actually
sprinted out from the dorm and dived into
the lake with all my clothes on. I got into real
bother for it. Afterwards, I couldn't think why
I'd done it. Except to say that my heart was far
away in Devon.*

*But now I may have worried you, Emma,
with talk of jumping into lakes in the middle*

*of the night! There's nothing to be concerned
about. Olivier had me out in a jiffy – he
understood, of course – and no one would have
been any the wiser if it hadn't been for that
creep Perkins telling tales to gain favour with
the masters. A chap needs a true friend here and
Olivier is the truest. Only one more year in this
unfeeling place and if all goes well, he and I will
be off to the gleaming spires of Oxford!*

*What are you reading today, Em? I think of
you looking out over the rooftops of London.
Does it weary you, staying hidden away
from all the world? I know you could never
be lonely with all your books, but I wonder
if Mother would not want you to experience
life? And so, don't be shocked – I'm going to
smuggle you out for a trip when I come back at
Christmas! There's something I must see and
I insist you come with me. I've heard that a
great tiger was shot in the jungles of India by
Lord Ripon and gifted to the Natural History
Museum. The tiger's name is Bhayankar
Raaja, Fierce King. He prowled his jungle
territory, ever watchful, protecting his realm.*

*He was legendary. I'd like to see him, to look
into his eyes, see his great paws and—*

The writing became blurred here and she couldn't
make out the rest of the sentence. She skipped to
where the writing became legible again.

> *I promise, I will keep you safe. Say you will
> come, Em.*
> *Now, onto other matters, how's your
> knitting these days? Are you coming on? I
> caught a terrible cold from my swim and it's
> always freezing here. Would you make me a
> scarf? You must knit it in the brightest orange,
> with black and white stripes, so you would
> easily find me if I should ever be lost.*
> *With all my very best love, darling little sister.*
> *Yours,*
> *James Linden*

Emma frowned at the letter. No mention of the
grisly moment they'd come across that man, the
morning they left Kersbrook. He'd been fetching
his trap from the boundary hedge, a stoat caught

between its iron jaws. James demanded the poor creature from him and sent the man, whoever he was, packing. But it was already dead, lolling against James's palm, its blood smeared across his fingertips. Despite her horror, Emma had been awed by the poise of its tiny head, and the neat, muscular body.

'Hunted as vermin,' James whispered, his face whiter than bone. 'Fiercely territorial... like little tigers.'

They'd buried it with ceremony beside the bay tree and he'd barely spoken the whole train journey back to London.

He'd been deeply disturbed by the creature's death. Why did he not mention it? Perhaps he was being careful, knowing Father read his letters. But there was this strange talk of a tiger and an outlandish plan for an impossible outing! That was not being careful. Why would he write it so plainly, as if to purposely land himself in hot water? It made no sense.

'Emma.'

Her father's voice sent ice pouring through her veins.

'What are you doing here? Turn around and answer me.'

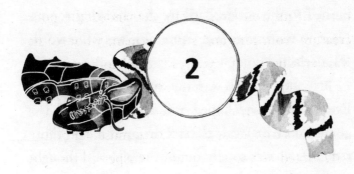

*Devon, Summer Term 2023*

The Jurassic Coast contains 185 million years in ninety-six miles of English coastline, like a timeline in rock, but don't ask me anything else about it. All I know is that I live at the oldest end, where the cliffs are red and date back to the Triassic Period. And I only know *that* because my football academy team, the Raptors, was named after the *eoraptor*, one of the first dinosaurs to evolve in the Late Triassic. Apparently.

On the day I found Rosie Linden standing on top of a litter bin in the middle of the high street, I was supposed to be at the club training with the other Raptors. But earlier that morning, before I'd even put down my kitbag, I'd found my name on a list pinned to the noticeboard by the changing rooms. Next to my name, *Jude Simmons*, were the words 'Not selected'.

Just like that, I was out of football academy. Everything I had hoped and trained so hard for, gone. Coach may as well have dropped me off those red cliffs. It was totally out of the blue. I'd thought I was well on my way to becoming a pro. It was everything I'd dreamed of.

So I'd bolted, slamming through the fire exit. Out of the building. Out of the club grounds. Out of the Raptors, for ever. *Not selected. Not selected.* The words roared in my head. I didn't know where I was going, I just found myself running all the way back to town. And there was Rosie, standing on a litter bin outside the pound shop, wobbling slightly as she looked up at the sky.

Rosie Linden, a girl in my class, missing for four days and four nights. Everyone had been worried about her. And here she was, surrounded by a crowd.

It took me a moment to recognise her. Normally she has this bouncy, curly hair with a life of its own. She's always on about the environment, saving tigers, turtles or elephants. A while ago, she had us signing a petition to stop some woods nearby being chopped down for a new road and recently, she'd been handing out leaflets about a march in London. Something to do with climate change. But up on that bin, her hair was flat with grease and dirt. Her clothes were filthy, like she'd been crawling in mud. I could see her fingernails were caked in it.

'It's the girl from the news,' someone said. 'They had the helicopter out looking for her.'

But it was like Rosie couldn't see them staring. She carried on looking up at the sky, as if searching for something.

'I've called the police,' said someone else. 'They're on their way.'

'Don't go near her. There's something not right with her,' a man with a bald head said.

'She's lost it,' said a teenage girl, standing with her friends. 'She's absolutely lost it.' And they started mimicking Rosie, laughing.

I took a deep breath. My mum's a nurse, and she 'interferes' all the time. That's what she calls it. She says she can't help herself. And things happen around her. It's like people see her coming and think, *Right, it's safe to be ill now, she'll take care of me.*

Wherever Mum goes, they collapse, slice open their fingers or have an asthma attack. And she's there like a shot, 'interfering', putting their feet in the air or telling them to stay calm and feeling for a pulse.

That's the problem with having a mum like mine. You're never short of knowing what you *should* do. She would never have walked past Rosie and not tried to help. Plus, I'd seen Rosie's mum on the news, pleading for Rosie to come home, hardly able to get her words out she was crying so hard.

I walked through the crowd.

'Hey, don't get too close, son. She might get violent,' called the man with the bald head.

'That's right, very unpredictable they are. Leave it to the professionals,' said a woman.

'They kept 'em separate in my day,' muttered an old man. 'Now they go wherever they like and it's every other day you see a headline of someone getting stabbed by a crazed lunatic.'

I turned and glared at him. I couldn't help it. Unless he was about to take up poaching rhinos for their horns or illegal logging of the rainforest, he didn't have anything to fear from Rosie. I couldn't

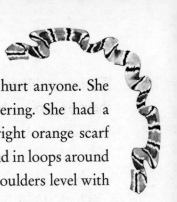

see how they thought she would hurt anyone. She looked skinny and she was shivering. She had a T-shirt and leggings on, and a bright orange scarf with white and black stripes, wound in loops around her neck. I stood below her, my shoulders level with her trainers.

'Hey, Rosie,' I called, squinting against the sun.

She didn't pay any attention. It was as though she hadn't heard.

'Rosie. It's Jude from school.' It occurred to me she might not know who I was. We only share one subject. Had we actually ever spoken? 'Jude Simmons. I'm in your English class. I play a lot of football.' Played, I should have said. Past tense. I play*ed* a lot of football. The memory was like being smashed in a nasty tackle, but I couldn't think about it right then.

She looked around but not at me. Her whole body was tense with concentration. What was she searching for?

'Rosie?'

I could feel the eyes of the crowd drilling holes in my back and wondered how long it would take for the police to come. There was a bench next to the bin, so I hopped onto it. Maybe if I got in her line of sight, she would hear me. Up close, her face was speckled with dirt. Dry tracks ran down her cheeks where she'd been crying.

'Rosie, it's Jude from school. Can you hear me?'

She seemed so lost in her own thoughts, it was like I wasn't there at all.

My mum has this thing where she says we don't touch each other enough. She's told me about old people who go to the hairdressers more than they need to, because it's the only time they feel close to another human being. In her opinion, what most people need is a big hug. It's something to do with a hormone called oxytocin that's released in your brain. Mum says we need hugs like we need vitamins. She gets hold of me in the morning, flings her arms around me and counts to thirty. That's how long it takes to start the oxytocin flowing. Then I have to tell her to get off. My mum would do that all day if I let her. That's how much she believes in the goodness of hugs.

I definitely wasn't going to hug Rosie in front of all these people. Apart from anything else, I might accidentally knock her off the bin. I imagined what

Mum might do if she was here. Maybe if I got hold of Rosie's hand, very gently, she might notice me.

I reached out and it was like magic. She jolted and looked round, but I could tell that she didn't recognise me. Her eyes were darting all over the place, as if she was spotting things in the sky above my head. I had to stop myself from turning to look, though I knew there was nothing there.

Something was *really* wrong with her.

'Rosie, everyone's looking for you. Your mum's worried.'

She seemed to hear that time. She looked at my hand holding hers. I suddenly realised this might be weird for her. But I remembered what Mum had told me about touch. It felt important not to let go of Rosie. As if letting go would break the connection, like cutting off a phone call.

'Rosie, I'm in your class at school.' I wracked my brains for ordinary things to say. 'I'm in Mrs Wright's class with you. My name's Jude Simmons, but probably you don't know me because I spend all my time playing football.'

She gave me a thin smile. I felt like I could hear Mum's voice say, *Good, keep going, Jude.*

'You're best friends with Imogen, aren't you? Imogen Richards. We live on the same street. She's number forty-two and I'm at thirty-one.'

Me and Imogen have known each other since we were babies. There's a photo of me naked in the bath with her and her brothers when we were about three. Imogen is the prettiest girl in our year. A few months ago, after I turned thirteen, I realised she was pretty *and* that I'd had naked baths with her, and it was just too weird. So now I feel awkward around her and we don't really speak any more.

Rosie nodded slowly but it was as if she was only half-listening, like talking to someone with their headphones in.

'Rosie, will you sit down on the bench with me? My legs are tired from football practice this morning.'

That was a lie. If my legs were tired, it was from running away from the club as fast as they would carry me. Running from shame and anger and disappointment. But I didn't tell her that.

'You're tired?' Her voice was croaky. She looked concerned for me.

'Yeah, really tired, Rosie.' Still lying.

She nodded and let me help her off the bin. The crowd gave a cheer but I ignored them and hoped Rosie would too. She didn't seem to notice. She sat down, holding on tightly to my hand. This close, I had to hold my breath. She smelled of stale sweat and rubbish. What had she been doing for the last four days?

As if reading my thoughts, she leaned in and whispered, 'Don't worry, Jude. I've been protecting you all. Guarding you. Keeping you safe.'

*London, September 1884*

Before she knew what she was doing, Emma crumpled James's letter into her pocket.

'I came to say goodbye to you, Father,' she said, spinning around. The ease of the lie took her by surprise.

As did the expression that flickered across his face. For the briefest of moments, she saw panic and fear – deep down she'd known showing emotion would distract him, but to see him made afraid by it shocked her.

He recovered quickly, his features as impassive as ever. 'Silence, solitude and rational thought, Emma. Farewells are illogical sentimentality. I travel for business and I return. I will speak to the doctors about this troubling slip of yours.' He reached for the bell cord. 'Wait on the landing for Mrs Carter to escort you upstairs.'

The letter burning like a hot coal in her pocket, Emma hurried from the room, her pulse hammering in her ears.

The housekeeper's grip was like a vice on Emma's wrist.

'Well, you've caused a right old upset, young lady, I don't mind telling you. I've never seen your father so keen to get out of the house and *that's* saying something.'

She half-dragged Emma up the stairs. Emma bit back her tears. Another display of emotion was not going to help. If anything, she was relieved to go back to the attic. It was safest for everyone that she obeyed the doctors' rules.

Mrs Carter strode into the room, pulling Emma round sharply so she stood facing her. The bunch of keys at the housekeeper's waist jangled as she reached into her apron, pulling out the familiar murky brown glass bottle and a tablespoon.

'Better double dose you, after your morning's antics. And all the things I have to do today, what with your father off on his travels again and Mrs Rowlands retiring.'

Emma gulped down the bitter medicine from the spoon. Mrs Rowlands had been the cook for as long as Emma could remember.

Mrs Carter nodded with satisfaction. 'You have put yourself in terrible danger. I hope you understand the seriousness of what you've done?'

Emma nodded.

The woman turned on her heel and marched out of the door, shutting it smartly behind her.

Emma collapsed into her chair, her face hot with shame. Mrs Carter was right, she'd put herself in danger. She hoped the medicine would work soon, and soothe the churning in her stomach. Rubbing her wrist she gazed around the old nursery, high up under the eaves. Here, in the attic of number two, Chelsea Gardens, Old Brompton Road, London, twelve-year-old Emma Linden lived and never went out.

The tools to discipline her mind and control her mental sickness were all around her. Emma's scientific drawings of shells, plants and fossils feathered the walls like the flank of a great bird. Piles of books on biology, chemistry and geology jostled for space on every surface, the bookcase long since full. On top of a teetering stack on her bedside table was her favourite; well-thumbed, the title, *The Life of Mary Anning*, nearly rubbed from the spine. Mary Anning, the famous fossil-hunter, had lived not far from the red cliffs in Devon, near Kersbrook.

Only Emma's desk was clear. The desk had belonged to her mother. Made of dark mahogany, the table folded away into a hidden compartment and inside was the drawer where she had discovered her ammonite. The legs were carved with swirling patterns, inlaid with droplets of mother of pearl. James always said it had been made for a relative of Mother's, a sea captain with the East India Company. She stroked the polished wood with a shaking palm.

Her mother had died shortly after Emma was born. She knew little about her. The desk was her only connection and Emma clung to it, as if it might reveal something about her. Instinctively, she felt for the secret message carved on the inside of one of the legs. She had found the writing not long after Timothy the footman had fetched the desk from Father's study. He'd eased it up the narrow staircase one rainy day in March, huffing and blinding under his breath. Father's decision to move the desk had taken everyone by surprise. It seemed such a thoughtful act. Then Timothy brought the matching chair, but he didn't stay long. It was unlikely Emma's condition was contagious, but it was better to be safe than sorry.

If Emma hadn't dropped a slide from her microscope a week or so later, she might never have come across the words. Smoothed by age, they had clearly been there for many years. Now, she ran her fingers over the familiar sentence.

*I will keep you safe.*

It felt like a promise, as though her mother were watching over her.

But there was no promise strong enough to save her from Father's displeasure if he knew she had stolen James's letter. She uncrumpled it from her pocket.

It was so odd. His tone was like someone caught up in the excitement of his own thoughts.

She didn't believe he had given any consideration to Father reading it. This was strange in itself. James was all too aware of Father's high standards, and strove to achieve them. It was the talk of the tiger that niggled most, like an unbalanced chemical formula. And no mention of the stoat. She frowned. The expression on the man's face rose in her mind, his moustache quivering, his cold, hard stare, a look of pure hatred levelled at her brother. He'd left without argument but it might have gone differently if Olivier hadn't been there.

Emma shivered and stared out at the grey London rooftops. She wished she could see James. His school felt a long way away and Christmas even further.

Leaving the attic had been worth the risk, if only to keep Father from reading the letter. And – a new thought struck her – nothing bad had happened. She'd left the attic and there'd been no fit. She placed her fingers at her wrist and took her pulse. Normal. She laid her hand on her chest. Her breathing was… normal.

*Devon, Summer Term 2023*

I stared at Rosie, trying to keep calm, but my heart was pounding. What was I supposed to say? Protecting us all from what? How could Rosie guard anyone from anything? She couldn't even look after herself.

I live at number thirty-one, Harewood Road. At number twenty-nine lives our neighbour, Walter. Walter's ninety-three or something like that. He's got Alzheimer's disease. It makes you forget things and it happens a lot to elderly people. Walter forgets that he's already told you something, so you have to act as if it's the first time you've heard it or he gets upset. Sometimes he forgets he's an old man and tells me about his new baby son, David. Well, David is sixty-two and an investment banker in

London. But the best thing for Walter is to go along with what he says. My mum's amazing at it. When Walter tells her about baby David, she hugs him (I told you, she loves hugs) and says congratulations. She asks how much David weighs and when he's coming home from the maternity unit. She tells him she can't wait to meet him and isn't a new baby a wonderful thing? Mum says you've got to enter Walter's world. So it was Walter I was thinking about when I decided to enter Rosie's world.

'Protecting us? Wow, that was brave of you. Thank you.'

She nodded and I could see her relax a bit.

'Have you been guarding us the whole time you've been away?'

She nodded again. 'Yes. I've kept you safe.'

'Have you eaten or had any sleep, while you've done all that protecting?'

She shook her head. There was a cereal bar in my rucksack. I wondered if she would be okay with me getting it out of my bag.

Suddenly she sat up straight and looked into the sky. I'd lost her again. It was frightening to see her disappear inside herself like that. I held tight to her hand, but my grip must have hurt her because she looked at me sharply, a furious glare on her face.

'Let go of me! You don't understand. It's in my nature to protect. I have to go. You'll regret it if you try to hold onto me.'

I tried to stay calm but inside I was panicking. I was so out of my depth. One of the crowd had said they'd called the police, so where were they? I didn't want to hurt Rosie, but what else could I do to keep her there until someone came to help?

I thought of Mum and what she might say. 'You know, before a big game, professional footballers have a rest day. It's part of their training regime.'

'Let go of me!' She tried to wrench her hand away, but I held on.

'Rosie, your guarding duties are like a big football match. If you want to be the best, you have to take a break and some time out…'

She was staring at me now.

'It's to do with muscle fibres,' I went on. 'I can't remember exactly, but they need time to repair after exercise, to build stronger muscles. And you have to eat and drink well too.'

I was totally making it up, but it sounded like

what I'd been told at the academy. 'You can't do a good job of protecting us unless you've had a drink. And a rest.'

I could tell she was considering what I'd said.

'I've got a cereal bar in my bag. Would you like it?'

She hesitated, then nodded.

I didn't really want to let go of her hand but I had to get my bag off my back. I passed her the cereal bar and my water bottle. She tried to pretend she wasn't bothered, but she pretty much inhaled the cereal bar and then downed my water in big, thirsty gulps.

'Now I have to go.' She turned her head as if someone was calling her from a distance.

'Wait, Rosie.' I took her hand again, glancing quickly around. No sign of the police. Surely they'd be here any minute. If I could just keep her there. 'You haven't rested. Ten minutes should do it. Remember, you need to rest to be better at guarding.'

Already she looked better for having had something to eat and drink.

'Come on, Rosie. Sit here.'

She sighed. 'All right, but just ten minutes.'

She slumped back on the bench next to me. Most people had moved on, except for a few stragglers who stared from a distance. The sun was warm on our faces, but I couldn't relax. Rosie's head began to droop and by degrees, came to rest on my shoulder. I concentrated on a stitch that had come loose in her orange scarf. I didn't dare move a muscle. Her breathing was slow and steady. I reckoned she had fallen asleep. She must have been exhausted. Four days and four nights. It wasn't a hug, but I wondered if you could get an oxytocin burst by putting your head on someone's shoulder. I hoped so. Rosie needed one of those.

It wasn't long after Rosie had fallen asleep that the paramedic arrived in her green overalls. Placing her medical bag on the ground, she crouched beside me and introduced herself.

'Hey, I'm Alice and I'm a paramedic,' she whispered.

I can't explain it, but there was something about her that made me feel everything was going to be okay. She was clean and capable-looking and I could tell she would stay calm in a zombie attack. I have never been so pleased to see anyone in my life.

'Someone gave us a call.'

I nodded, trying not to move my shoulder in case I disturbed Rosie, but it was no good. She sat up groggily.

I put on a fake, cheery voice. I knew I had to keep things normal or Rosie would be gone.

'Hi, Alice, I'm Jude and this is Rosie. She's been working really hard to protect us and that's why she's been missing for a few days. She's just having a quick rest, then she's got to get on with guarding.'

I hoped Alice would understand I didn't believe all that, but it was the story I'd used to get Rosie to stay. And because Alice turned out to be totally amazing, she got it straight away.

'Oh yeah, it's really important to rest and here's me coming along and disturbing your sleep. Sorry.' She smiled at Rosie.

What happened next is a bit of a blur. There was a kind policeman called Jeff, and Alice's shift partner, Phil. Somehow Alice persuaded Rosie to get in the ambulance. She went, sort of shyly, keeping a tight grip so that I ended up in there too.

Out of sight, I overheard Jeff ask Phil, 'What do you reckon? Maybe schizophrenia?'

I only just caught Phil's reply, his voice was so low. 'Could be any number of mental health conditions that have symptoms like this, but maybe schizophrenia.' Then he appeared round the edge of the door and spoke quietly in Alice's ear. 'Hospital's on OPEL 4. There's not a bed free in the whole place and the emergency department's bursting at the seams.'

'She'd be better off at home, anyway,' Alice replied.

'I dunno, but doesn't look like we've got a choice.'

'Come on, you know hospital's not the best place for someone this fragile. She needs her family.'

'All right, I'll let the duty psychiatrist know the address and we can meet the crisis team there.' He strode off again, and reappeared a second later, leaping into the ambulance cab, reaching for the radio. And all the while, Rosie hung onto me like an anchor in a storm.

5

*London, September 1884*

Three days later, Emma sneaked out from the attic again. She reasoned she was testing a hypothesis. It was an entirely rational expedition, so she should come to no harm. But she couldn't deny the tingle of excitement as she crept along the corridor. She had no particular destination in mind. Her aim was to study the results.

The flump of pillows hitting the floor made Emma pause outside one of the bedrooms. She spied Tilly changing the bedding through the crack between the hinges. When she moved towards the door, a pile of sheets in her arms, Emma fled upstairs, and sat on her chair.

Now to wait and observe any effects.

One minute, two minutes… Her breathing eased.

Five, ten… She checked her pulse.

Normal.

After twenty minutes, when there had been no fit, she slowly smiled.

Emma felt bolder. On the next occasion, she watched Timothy winding the clocks. It made her want to laugh out loud – he had no idea she was there. She slipped softly down the stairs.

Mrs Carter's voice made her freeze, mid-step.

'Now, Elspeth, Mr Linden asked me to speak plainly. He was glad to take my recommendation of you, being assured of your trustworthiness. Mrs Rowlands's retirement left him in quite a quandary. He dislikes taking on new staff due to the delicate nature of the household.'

Delicate nature? Emma frowned. Who was the housekeeper speaking to? She crept closer to the parlour door, tucking herself behind a thick curtain.

A woman's voice replied, 'Don't worry yourself on that account, Agnes. I keep the strictest of confidences. I'm glad to have found somewhere so well-paid, thanks to you.'

It must be the new cook. Tilly had said she was starting today – an old friend of Mrs Carter's.

'Well, Elspeth, here's how it stands. Mr Linden's daughter is of very fragile health.'

Emma bit her lip to stop herself gasping. They were talking about her!

'She is afflicted with a malady of the mind which comes from her mother's side – ran in the family like a seam of coal. Mrs Linden died shortly after Miss Emma was born. Not here, of course, supposedly in an *asylum*.' There was a pause. Mrs Carter would be crossing herself, as she always did on the rare occasion she spoke of Mother. What was an asylum? Mother had died at home. Hadn't she?

Emma bit her lip again, alarmed – Mother had *died* from this sickness, and here she was playing silly games, putting herself in danger. After all her father and the doctors had done to keep her safe. *What* was she doing?

*Silence, solitude, rational thought.* She shifted to return to the attic, but what else might Mrs Carter say? Instead, Emma squeezed the ammonite. It

34

reminded her of her books and her microscope slides in the attic. The world continued to orbit the sun as it had always done. The thought steadied her.

Mrs Carter continued. 'It was hoped the children had not inherited the illness, but Emma suffered a knock to the head when she was small. I was not with the family then, but I'm told she clean lost all reason, and drifted into a prolonged fit. It was clear Emma shared her mother's mental disease.'

Emma swallowed hard. She had no memory of the fall down the stone steps outside Uncle Henry's house and only the tiniest of snippets of the aftermath. James's face took on a haunted look when she once asked about it, so she'd never dared ask again. Whatever she had become in those moments, it had terrified him.

'A strict regime of plain diet, confinement and study is what the doctors prescribe. But it only delays the inevitable – one day the condition will manifest itself, and there isn't much that can be done. Mr Linden will not even suffer Emma to have a governess for fear of too much social stimulation, which puts a great deal of extra strain on me, I don't mind telling you. The doctors prescribe a trip to the coast each summer to take the sea air, which gives us all some relief.'

Emma closed her eyes at the thought of Kersbrook. It had always been in Mother's family. If you were to fly above Kersbrook like a bird, the house would look like a capital E written on the ground. The upright stroke of the E faced the lane, while the prongs looked out over the garden and fields beyond. At the back, a glass conservatory nestled, facing west, a warm spot to watch the last rays of sun on a summer's evening. Both James and Emma called it their 'perfect house'.

'The truth is, we are a little afraid of the child. Still, it's my Christian duty to have compassion, and I know a good-hearted woman like yourself, Elspeth, will feel the same.'

Emma didn't hear the reply. She felt sick. They were afraid of her? Afraid of the madwoman she would become. Just like her mother. Is that why their mother's life was shrouded in mystery? Mrs Carter's tone indicated an asylum, whatever that was, was not a place you'd go willingly. Is this what lay ahead for Emma? One day the sickness would take over, she would be consumed in a fit of madness and nothing would bring her back.

In the parlour, the conversation went on. 'Between you and me, Mr Linden travels as much as he does because Emma is a constant reminder of his sorrow and shame. I am told she takes after her mother in appearance and temperament. No wonder he keeps her at arm's length, knowing what is coming.'

Emma felt like a specimen. It was something to hear your own history described so bluntly to a stranger.

'I understand he was once a charming young man, but you will find Mr Linden reserved and devoted to his business interests, which will one day be passed on to his young son. Master James is away at school and has excellent prospects. He is to take a place at Oxford. We are all very proud of him, and so handsome and pleasing. Praise God, Master James has been spared Emma's troubles. I can't think what will become of her.'

She'd heard enough. Emma tiptoed back to the attic and sat down at her desk, surveying the horizon.

'Wind's north, five to seven,' she whispered. 'Sea's moderate. Weather's fair. Visibility's good. Excellent. Raise the anchor...'

With a shaking hand, she dipped her pen into the pot of ink, then made a mark on the page in front of her. For at least the millionth time, she imagined the grey London rooftops were the choppy swell of the Atlantic, her desk the prow of a great ship, and her pen plotting the course of a scientific expedition, like Darwin or Magellan. Over the sea, and far, far away.

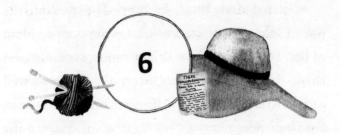

## 6

*London, December 1884*

Voices carried up the stairs, Mrs Carter shouting at Tilly.

'For goodness' sake, girl, get the bell!'

Emma turned to the sheaf of papers propped up on her desk. James's distinctive handwriting leaped across each of them.

She hadn't replied immediately. She'd first sent him the scarf he'd asked for. Mrs Carter had been shocked at the colour of the wool. Orange? Stripes? In the end, her approval of Emma knitting, Mrs Carter's own favourite pastime, won her round.

But eventually Emma did write back. She couldn't go with him to see the tiger. It was impossible. Out of the question. Couldn't Olivier accompany him? Why did she need to go?

In letter after letter, he tried to persuade her; with Father away on business, they came safely to her, sometimes three or four in a week. Yes, he wrote, Olivier would join them, but James wanted Emma to come too. Was she not tired of staying in the attic? Was she not curious to see the tiger? She wouldn't be alone. It would be no different to going to Devon. In fact, with the three of them together, it would be *just* like the summer.

From one envelope, a newspaper clipping fluttered to the floor. It was a cutting from *The Times*. 'British Soldier in Tiger Transformation' read the headline. Emma scanned the text in bewilderment.

The young man was found in a state of great self-neglect in a forest clearing in the Garo Hills, north-eastern India. He had been missing from his barracks for four days. He believed he had been a tiger, protecting the forest from the British Raj's felling programme. Winching equipment at various sites in the area was sabotaged over several nights during the same period, however officials report the damage was so severe that the soldier could not be responsible and it was more likely caused by local rebel forces. British Magistrate, Mr J. Elliot, who has travelled widely in the area, suggested the young man fell victim to fanciful ideas after hearing local Garo folklore. He reports, 'Among the Garo, a madness exists which they call tiger transformation. Local stories tell of Rai Bagh, a Garo king, who could turn himself into a tiger.' Medical doctors believe the soldier was suffering from the heat. He has returned to Delhi to convalesce and is expected to make a full recovery.

She shook her head. What stories! A person turning into a tiger? But James's letter was full of the article.

'Imagine your hands turning into great paws in front of your eyes,' he wrote. 'Imagine being at one with the forest. Incredible! Please come and see Bhayankar Raaja.'

Slowly James's doggedness began to chip away at her resolve and made her wonder if, maybe, she shouldn't go. If one day the sickness would come anyway, why not…?

Then, in the first week of December, James hit on the thing that might convince her to take such an enormous risk. The tiger would be interesting, of course, but there was another reason Emma should visit the Natural History Museum... a very special fossil was on display there. The museum had been open three years and among its treasures were the remains of a creature Emma had only ever dreamed of seeing, until now.

Her tummy had been fizzing with fear and anticipation for days. Today was their only chance. If he missed his train... If there was a delay... After such raised expectations, Emma didn't think she could bear it if something should stop them from going.

'Mister James! Take those muddy boots off this minute!' Mrs Carter's voice was drowned out by the thundering of feet on the stairs. Emma jumped up. James! At last!

'Em!' He burst into the room, gathering her up in a hug, then pushing away to look at her. 'You have grown… again! I will not have it.' He laughed. 'You are not to change without my permission!'

She beamed. It was wonderful to have him home. The house came alive when he was there. 'And how was your journey? I worried you might be held up.'

'Fine. Fine.' He waved her questions away. 'Now, look at this, I have bought you a book.'

He offered a parcel wrapped in brown paper.

'What is this, James?'

'It's about the Danish naturalist, Peter Wilhelm Lund.' James ripped apart the paper in his eagerness. 'He discovered the sabre-toothed tiger fossil.'

Tigers again. What was this obsession?

'Say you like it.'

'I do, I do.' She smiled, turning the volume over in her hands. It was a beautiful book, bound in soft green leather, embossed golden tendrils and leaves framing the title.

'But Mary Anning remains your favourite?'

She grinned. Mary's most famous discovery was, right this minute, not many metres from Emma's front door, and it was the reason she'd finally agreed to go along with James's wild plan.

Mary Anning's *ichthyosaur* fossil was said to have changed the course of science. It was dismissed as a fake, then as a crocodile, but Mary discovered a dinosaur skeleton before anyone even believed in dinosaurs. Emma was fascinated by this remarkable woman. Mary's family were poor so she had barely been to school, unlike the scholarly men who took credit for her discoveries and excluded her from their learned academies. And yet, Mary persevered, teaching herself and excavating fossils from the cliffs after wild storms. It wasn't just the *ichthyosaur* that made Emma want to go. She felt a bond with Mary: another woman, separate from society, working in pursuit of science. To be in the presence of one of Mary's *own* finds, Emma felt certain, would be life changing.

James grinned back at her. 'Now, there's no time to lose. This is our only chance. It's Mrs Carter's afternoon off and Father is not due home until this evening. They will never know.' He delved into a sack he'd brought with him, bringing out a wide-brimmed floppy hat, and plopped it on her head. 'No one can see your face unless they come up close.' He peaked under the brow of the hat. 'Perfect.'

'You really think it will be all right for me to leave the house…?' Emma's voice trailed off, nerves giving her second thoughts now the moment had come.

He gazed solemnly at her. 'I do, Emma. You come to Devon every summer. Surely that journey is much more dangerous to your health than a short walk down the street? Life is for living. Besides, I'll take good care of you, I promise.'

She smiled up at him. She knew he would.

He draped a long coat over her shoulders and laughed. 'You could pass for an elderly aunt!'

The bottom of the coat brushed the floor, heavy and awkward. But she laughed too, hobbling around the attic in her disguise, doing her best impression of an imaginary great aunt. James's enthusiasm was infectious. It was an expedition after all. A real one, at long last. No one would recognise her. James and Olivier would be with her. What could possibly go wrong?

He bent down so she could re-tie the orange scarf around his neck. There was something about his expression, a tension that made his smile seem put on for her benefit. They locked eyes.

'Just a little tired, that's all, Em.' He grasped her hand before she could say anything, pulling her out of the room.

On the landing, James put a finger to his lips, and they paused, listening. 'Mrs Carter had her coat on so she should be gone by now,' he whispered.

The coast was clear. Emma followed him carefully down the stairs.

Tilly was absorbed in setting the fire in the dining room as they sneaked past. At the back door James slid the bolts in their lock while Emma kept lookout for Timothy. He eased it open, and daylight flooded the hallway. Emma froze, shielding her eyes. It had been weeks since she'd left the attic, let alone the house.

The din of traffic and people reached her ears. Carriages clattered and street hawkers shouted. So much noise. Her heart thudded. She couldn't move a muscle even if she wanted to.

James tugged at her arm. 'Come on, Emma.'

She stared wildly at him. She couldn't do it. Instinctively she shoved her hand into the coat pocket, but her ammonite was buttoned up under the layers of her disguise.

46

James glanced hurriedly over his shoulder, back into the airless darkness of the house. The tension she had noticed was now etched across his face.

'Don't let me down. I can't... I won't go without you.' He pulled at her arm again. 'I know! Think of yourself as Mary Anning, out on the cliffs hunting for fossils! Think of how she stood up to those men of science who told her she was wrong.'

Emma closed her eyes. Mary's *ichthyosaur* was just a short walk away. She took a deep breath and stepped on to the pavement. With each stride bolstered by the thought of Mary's determination, she marched arm-in-arm with James all the way to the museum.

7

'James! Emma!'

Olivier, James's best friend, and so dear to Emma, met them by the entrance. 'Emma, you look a treat in that get-up!'

'It's so good to see you, Olivier.' Emma knew no one like him. His family were French and he had been born in Tangiers, in Morocco. With his accent, his charm, his kindness – he had always seemed a little magical.

'Come on then, we have a tiger to see. Honestly, Emma, he's been going on about this for weeks.' Olivier's smile didn't quite reach his eyes.

Through the great doors, beyond the foyer, high-ceilinged corridors and halls echoed with the throng of crowds. Emma stared about her. The museum was built to house one of the most extensive collections of natural history in the world. It was wondrous!

'There it is.' James let go of her arm, and pushed forward, shoving people roughly out of the way. 'Come on, Em...'

She turned to Olivier in alarm. It wasn't like James to be rude, even in his excitement.

Olivier took her arm as they followed, a strained look on his face, offering apologies to those left reeling in James's wake. Embarrassed, Emma kept her head down, but she was growing hotter and hotter under her hat, her shoulders aching from the weight of the coat. Wool fibres itched her bare forearms. She longed to pull it off, shake her head and breathe.

And then she saw the tiger.

Bhayankar Raaja. He was magnificent, or rather, he had been. The taxidermist had set his mouth in an awkward grimace, probably to make him look as if he was roaring. The sight horrified her. Bhayankar Raaja should never have been brought to wet, grey London. He should have been left to live deep in his jungle kingdom, not reduced to this faded and cheapened Bhayankar Raaja. The tiger before her was nothing but a hollow sham.

She glanced at her brother. James had been so looking forward to this. He was fiddling with his collar, chewing on his thumbnail, eyes glued to the display. She was certain he understood the tragedy of this creature being stuffed and gawped at by school children, but he didn't say anything. None of them did.

Out of nowhere, a snotty-nosed boy leaned forward and poked the tiger in one of its glass eyes.

James clenched his fists, taking a step towards the boy. Emma and Olivier reached for James, both terrified he might strike him.

But with a shake of his head, Emma's brother turned and ran, pushing through the crowd even more roughly than when they'd arrived.

'Emma, come on,' Olivier said quickly.

They could barely keep up as he fled outside. They found him pacing the steps of the museum.

Hands clenched, James's eyes flickered over the stone slabs, as if following the scurrying of an army of ants.

He was so unlike himself, Emma felt suddenly afraid of him.

'Well, that was a bit of a disappointment, wasn't

it? Never mind. Let's go home for cake and tea.'
Only Olivier's voice was jolly.

James didn't seem to hear. This was more than disappointment.

'What do you say, James? I'm hungry, aren't you?' urged Olivier.

Still James paced, words shaping his lips soundlessly. Visitors to the museum eyed them curiously. Emma tried to ignore their stares. This was awful.

'James, let's go home, it's not far.' Olivier spoke gently and carefully now, but it was as though, for James, he didn't exist. She watched them from under the rim of her giant hat, at a loss as to what to say.

'Come, we have brought Emma out of the house,' Olivier pleaded. An officious-looking museum attendant was striding towards them. 'We must see she returns safely.'

Olivier placed his hand on James's arm, but he shook him off.

'Will you be quiet? I can't think with you all talking at once.' He jumped down the remaining steps and hailed a cab.

51

Terrified, Emma glanced at Olivier. His expression was grim.

'Hey there! Three fares.' James turned back to her. 'Emma – don't dawdle! Olivier, help her up, will you?' While he issued instructions to the driver, Emma climbed in. Oh, what a relief! They were going home.

Inside the cab, Emma leaned back on the padded seat, comforted by the sound of the horses' hooves clattering on the cobbles. It would only take a few minutes. She couldn't wait to be back in the safety of the attic.

Rocked by the motion of the turning wheels, she closed her eyes, a headache forming at her temples. The trip had been a disaster. She should never have agreed to it. What had come over James to behave so outrageously? She slowly opened her eyes. James was slumped in his seat, glowering out of the window, but Olivier sat bolt upright, glancing sharply at the passing landmarks.

'This isn't the way to Old Brompton Road. The driver's gone wrong.'

Now it was Emma's turn to sit up. She peered out of the window. This wasn't the route they had taken to the museum. They were going in the opposite direction!

'I'll tell the driver. He must have misheard you.' Olivier raised his arm to bang on the ceiling, but James grabbed hold of him, silently shaking his head.

'James, what's going on? We need to get Emma home.'

James winced and put his hands over his ears. 'Please... We *will* go home.' His voice was too loud, as though he were trying to make himself heard in a noisy room that was full of chatter. 'I promise. It isn't far. I just need to see...'

Tears pushed at the back of Emma's eyes. She was more frightened than she cared to admit. She took a deep breath and tried to imagine herself as Mary Anning, standing on the clifftop, ready to make new discoveries.

But her fears broke in. Had James forgotten the risk she had taken in coming? He'd promised to take care of her. It was all she could do to stop herself bursting into tears. So much for being an adventurer. She hadn't even seen Mary's *ichthyosaur*.

Olivier nodded. 'All right, James. But we go straight to Old Brompton Road afterwards.'

Emma gripped the edge of the seat. What if she had a fit as a result of the strain? She stared at them in shock. Yes, life was for living, but she wasn't ready to be mad yet, and the sickness could erupt at any moment.

Except... so far it hadn't, and she had already been under quite a lot of strain.

And something she couldn't begin to understand was happening to James.

These two thoughts niggled uneasily in her mind.

They travelled the rest of the way in silence, but Emma barely noticed. She had never been south of the river before. Crossing the Thames was intoxicating – so wide, fast and clogged with boats and shipping.

Beyond what she guessed must be Westminster Bridge, Emma studied the passing street names and stone buildings in awe. She'd never imagined London to be so huge.

At last, the cab stopped and they found themselves outside a vast building, fortified by endless iron railings. It was beginning to get dark. She watched James anxiously as he stared through the bars, chewing on his thumbnail. She followed his gaze up the towering pillars guarding the entrance, craning her neck to see the enormous domed roof looming over them. It seemed to be warning them not to enter.

'Where are we, James?' she asked, but he ignored her.

Emma couldn't imagine anybody living here. It looked so closed and empty, the windows barred and blank. A chill wind whisked along  the pavement, whipping up inside her coat. She shivered. A scrap piece of paper whirled past her boots and she thought suddenly of James's letters, filled with longing for their summers in Devon.  This strange place couldn't be more different to the welcoming cosiness of Kersbrook, its attic windows peeping like eyes in a smiling face from beneath the low-slate roof. Starfish and shell collections filling every windowsill, the beachcombing treasures of generations of children.

And the young man gripping the railings couldn't be more different to her brother. In Devon,

James's skin was bronzed by the sun, his hair glistening with sea spray. Now his face was pasty, his hair ashen, his shoulders sagging. He looked so pitiful, her heart reached out to him. On impulse, she slipped her hand in his.

'Do you know what this is, Em?' he asked, not taking his eyes from it.

She shook her head.

'Bethlem Royal Hospital. It's a lunatic asylum. It's where they lock up people who have gone mad. Bedlam, they call it.'

An asylum? Mrs Carter had said Mother died in an asylum. To Emma, hospitals meant clean white sheets and doctors with gold pocket watches, but that image didn't match this place.

'Do they make them better?'

'If you think that pulling out teeth, ice baths and doses of mercury to make a person vomit can cure madness, then yes, they make people better here.'

Emma felt sick. Did such things really happen? Is this where she would end up one day?

They stood in silence.

'Please, James, I want to go home.' She felt exhausted.

'Yes, it is late.' James nodded slowly.

'Come on, there's a cab coming our way.'

Olivier took charge, seeing them home and charming Mrs Carter with praise for the newly decorated Christmas tree while Emma sneaked upstairs. James was silent throughout. As if something inside had been switched off.

Before Olivier left, he came to the attic to say goodbye.

'Emma, my dear friend, I hope you see I had to go along with James's plan today, or he would have taken you by himself, and I needed to be sure you were both safe.'

He shook his head. 'It was no coincidence we were at Bethlem. I don't want you to be afraid. I've been reading a great deal and I must learn more, but I'm certain Bethlem is not somewhere you need concern yourself with. This is a passing phase with James. He will be his old self once he is away from that school, and I promise I'll see him through until then. I keep a close eye on him. I take him running whatever the weather and it does him no end of good. You know how much he loves to be active. Please, don't worry.'

Emma stared at Olivier, unable to make sense of it. A passing phase? He was trying to tell her something, to reassure her. But she *was* afraid, especially now she knew what an asylum was. It only deepened the mystery surrounding her mother. Worse, in her heart, Emma knew there was something very wrong with James. And so did Olivier.

*Devon, Summer Term 2023*

Every inch of wall space in Rosie's bedroom was covered with posters of endangered animals. One poster showed a tiger prowling the jungle. Text along the bottom said this was the Bengal tiger, photographed in the Garo Hills of India, and only 2,500 were left in the world. It made me think of my own bedroom and my football posters. They'd be coming straight down when I got home. To think I'd dreamed of appearing on a poster of my own one day. Somewhere between the Raptors noticeboard and the high street that morning, I'd decided I'd never be playing football again.

'Okay, Jude?' Alice put her hand on my shoulder. 'I think we can go now.'

Rosie's breathing was deep and regular. The medication had worked and she was asleep. She hardly made any shape under the duvet. Her grasp on my hand loosened as she drifted deeper into sleep.

Downstairs, Rosie's mum, Maddy, was with the nurse from the mental health crisis team who had met us when we first got back to Rosie's. Maddy's eyes were red-rimmed from days of worried crying. She had the same bouncy hair as Rosie, but it was streaked with grey. Rosie's stepdad, Rob, had dark circles under his eyes and was still wearing his work clothes, probably the ones he'd come home in the night Rosie went missing. He was a plumber. I knew that because I'd seen his van parked outside on the drive. Rosie's little brother, Eddie, was being taken care of by a friend. There were family photos of him around the lounge.

'We'll take Jude home now. His mum will be wondering where he's got to,' Alice said. I didn't put her right and tell her that Mum wouldn't be wondering at all. I wasn't supposed to finish at the academy for another hour yet.

'Thank you so much, Jude...' began Maddy,

60

trailing off in tears. She had a wodge of tissues in her hands, picking and pulling at them with her fingers.

Rob put a comforting arm around her shoulders.

'Aye, thanks for helping our Rosie this morning, Jude.'

I nodded and Alice led me out to the ambulance, where Phil was waiting in the cab. I don't think I was taking any of it in. I jumped into the middle seat and gave Alice directions to Harewood Road. As she took off the handbrake, I cleared my throat. 'So… this thing that's happening to Rosie.'

'Yeah…' Alice indicated left.

'She kept looking at things that weren't there. Like she could see another world inside ours.'

'That's an interesting way of putting it.'

I didn't know if that was good or bad, so I kept going.

'I know how people get physically ill,' I went on, questions buzzing around my head. 'Tummy bugs or breaking your arm.'

'Yeah…' Alice sounded like she was wondering where this was going. 'And you can be ill like that in your mind. You can be mentally ill, like you can be physically ill.'

But Rosie's illness had been different, it had been scary.

'So, what's the deal with Rosie? She *is* mentally ill, isn't she?'

I was aware of Alice and Phil exchanging a look over my head.

'Well…' Alice sounded like she wasn't keen on having this conversation. She took a deep breath. 'Look, I'm not supposed to discuss Rosie's health with anybody except Rosie and her family. Patient confidentiality and all that. But as you were there, I'll tell you that the doctor thinks Rosie might have had something called a psychotic episode. That's when a person's thinking and feelings become impaired. They lose contact with reality. They hear things or see things that aren't there, or believe things that aren't true. It's probably more common than you think.'

I watched the traffic streaming past the windscreen, my thoughts streaming just as fast.

'Sometimes it's brought on by a stressful event,' continued Alice. 'You might have heard in the media coverage that Rosie's gran died on Monday and apparently they were close.'

I had heard that on the radio.

'Really? Her gran dying might have caused Rosie to go off like that?'

'Well...' Alice shot Phil another look.

I thought I might be annoying her, but I didn't care – I needed to get my head round this. People's grannies die all the time and they don't act like Rosie did. My best friend Amin's grandad died last summer and they were tight as. But Amin didn't start seeing things that weren't there.

'It depends what else is happening in a person's life at the time. Rosie might have had an underlying mental illness no one knew about. Maybe her gran dying was the thing that brought it to the surface.'

I could tell she was being careful about what she said.

'I heard Maddy say there's a history of something like that in their family.'

'Well, sometimes a tendency can be passed down in families, no different to other illnesses, like diabetes or heart disease. But just because there's a tendency, doesn't mean it will definitely happen. That's when a trigger, like a stressful event in Rosie's case, might set off an underlying condition.'

We'd arrived outside my house. She switched the

engine off and put on a bright smile. 'Rosie will have lots of assessments and they'll work it out, although it might be a while before she's back at school. In the end, she'll be fine. People do get over things like this.'

'Okay.' I could see Walter peeking through his net curtains and hoped the sight of the ambulance wouldn't worry him. 'Great.' I didn't really know what she meant by 'assessments'. Was that great?

'Come on, I'll see you in,' said Alice. I think she was relieved to get me out of the cab so I wouldn't ask anything else. I leaped down after her.

When Mum answered the door and saw me standing with a paramedic, her jaw hit the floor.

'Oh my goodness! What's happened? Are you okay, Jude?'

'Nothing to worry about, Mrs Simmons. Your son has been a bit of a hero this morning,' said Alice.

Hero? Is that what they thought?

'Rosie Linden, the girl who's been missing. Jude found her on the high street. She's had some kind of mental breakdown. Jude was an absolute super star. He talked to her and kept her calm until we got there. Not many kids his age would have managed that.'

'Did he now?' Mum's face was proud but I could see she was confused. She doesn't miss anything.

I shrugged, avoiding eye contact.

'Absolutely. He's been brilliant.' Alice paused. 'It was a difficult situation. Look, I shouldn't really do this, but let me write my number down for you. Jude might have more questions about what happened.' Alice rummaged in her pockets and pulled out a pen and notepad.

I was surprised. Maybe it was okay to ask questions after all.

She passed me the paper. 'Leave a message if you don't get through and I'll call you.'

'Thank you. That's very kind… er…?' My mum faltered.

'Alice. I'm Alice Willard. And that's Phil.' She gestured back to the ambulance. 'Better get going, but well done, Jude.'

They waved as they drove off.

It took Mum precisely half a second after closing the front door. She got hold of my shoulders, looking me right in the face.

'Don't get me wrong, Jude, I'm really proud of you for helping your school friend. But what were you doing on the high street this morning? I dropped you off at football academy.'

The emotions of the day welled up inside me. 'Mum, I got dropped from the team. I didn't make the next stage of the squad.'

I started crying then. And because my mum is hands down the best mum in the whole, wide world, she didn't ask me any more questions. She just hugged me.

*London, November 1887*

It was Mrs Carter who woke Emma in the middle of the night. From under her mop cap, her grey hair hung over her shoulder in a long plait.

'Emma, wake up. Ill tidings. There are ill tidings. Now hurry.'

Mrs Carter helped her with her dressing gown and led her downstairs. The house was quiet, the only sound the ticking of the grandfather clock in the hall.

It was strange to remember that brief time, three years earlier, when she had broken the doctors' rules, creeping around the house on her own, and the disastrous outing to the museum. Emma had been all too glad to return to the safety of her studies in the attic.

In the drawing room, Mr Grant, Father's solicitor, sat in one of the upright chairs. A single lamp was lit, casting the room in shadow. Despite her dressing gown, Emma shivered. He jumped up when he saw her. Something was wrong.

'Mr Grant!'

She had known him since she was small. He had a grey moustache like that of a walrus, hanging over his top lip and obscuring his mouth. He was a kind man with a legion of grandchildren on whom he doted.

He reached out his hands to her.

'Emma. Sweet girl. My sincerest apologies for dragging you from your bed but oh, calamity, Emma. Calamity indeed.'

Her thoughts raced to James, and the memory of that difficult 'phase' as Olivier had called it, when he seemed so unlike himself. He had come through it, and was now thriving at university, his degree nearly complete. Still, the memory of Bethlem loomed in her mind. Ever since she had worried for him, worried about him, though she was never completely sure why.

'Your father, my dear...' Mr Grant hesitated, struggling for words.

She stared at him. Not James, then.

'There was a derailment. The train was travelling at speed along the edge of a narrow valley and ran off the rails. Your father... It was a tragic accident. Dreadful, my dear... I am more sorry than I can say.'

Emma turned cold. The shock was absolute.

'I must travel now to Oxford and inform your brother.' Mr Grant took up his hat. 'Such dreadful news. There is not a moment to lose. Your Uncle Henry will arrive in the morning to make arrangements, and both you and James need to be here. There are the businesses to think of. The board will want to know we have this all in hand.'

And with that he was off into the night.

Dazed, Emma allowed Mrs Carter to take her back to bed. She lay her head on the pillows.

Emma stared into the darkness. It didn't feel real. It couldn't be real. Father was a fixed landmark in her life. As fixed as Big Ben chiming the hours through the rest of that sleepless night, and just as remote. It was impossible that he could be gone.

James and Olivier returned with Mr Grant and were in the drawing room when she came down next morning.

'Emma.' James strode across the room and clasped her hands.

She saw her own shock and disbelief mirrored in his eyes.

Uncle Henry, Father's younger brother and partner in the family's mills and print works, was in the chair Mr Grant had sat in last night. The men's suits were black, like the dress Mrs Carter had laid out for her. They were all officially in mourning. Everything must be done properly.

Uncle Henry leaned forward, one elbow resting on the arm of the chair. His thick eyebrows gathered in one long line where his forehead furrowed. He had the presence of a politician delivering a speech on the steps of Downing Street. He explained what would now need to happen after Father's sudden death. His shares in the businesses would pass to James. Emma looked at her brother, standing with one arm around her shoulders. He seemed composed, in control. Only Olivier's watchful expression made her question it. His eyes were fixed on James's face.

It seemed Uncle Henry and Mr Grant had already worked out a plan. James should complete his studies. Uncle Henry would manage until James graduated that summer. Then he would come to London and begin work in the family firm.

Emma felt James stiffen. Across the room, she noticed Olivier clench his jaw, and look down at his boots.

Uncle Henry went on. Kersbrook would be sold since it had no practical use. Lord Holwell had expressed interest in purchasing it for his gamekeeper. It was a good location for the Holwell Estate.

Emma's hands flew to her face. Sell Kersbrook? Mother's family home! They couldn't! But it was as though she were in another room, invisible walls making it impossible for her to speak. She took a deep breath, slipping her hand into her pocket to feel for her ammonite, telling herself to stay calm.

'And what about Emma?' asked James, his voice taut.

Uncle Henry regarded her. 'Indeed, what to do with Emma.'

It was not a question, but the statement of a

problem. She could see she did not slot neatly into the machinery of her uncle's plans.

There was a brief silence before her uncle spoke.

'Do not worry yourself, Emma, my dear,' he said.

James squeezed her shoulder. She willed him to say something. His face was pale and drawn. What was he was thinking?

'I have a number of ideas how we may best settle your future,' Uncle Henry went on carefully, 'but we need not discuss them now. All in good time.'

She sat in stunned silence. Of all the thoughts crashing through her brain, it was the loss of Kersbrook, her beloved Kersbrook, that hurt her most. A precious link to their mother, and where she came alive for three months every summer. Did none of them realise what the place meant to her? What those few weeks of freedom meant to her? Did she not deserve some consideration? James stared ahead, his face blank. Even the weight of his arm felt insubstantial, like a shadow, as though he were somewhere else and his body an empty shell.

*Devon, Summer Term 2023*

If you can believe it, I kind of forgot what had happened with Rosie that Saturday. By Monday morning, all I could think about was the pitying looks and flack I was going to get from the other boys at school. Zak Riley especially. By now, they'd know I'd been dropped from the academy. *Not selected.* I'd built my whole life around football. What an idiot.

Amin was waiting for me at the school gates. Amin Dridi is my best friend for life. We met in pre-school by the car mat and we've been stuck together like glue ever since. He's taller than me, has an encyclopaedic knowledge of indie films, and likes to have cool designs shaved into the fade in his hair. In some ways we're quite different, but we always know what the other is thinking and we laugh at the same jokes. Up until recently, anyway.

'Mate, I heard about Saturday,' he said.

'I know you were never that bothered about it, but it was my whole world.'

Amin had tried out for the academy at the same time as me. He hadn't got in, but he wasn't worried. He does triathlon now. That's where there's three parts to the race: swimming, cycling and running. He's perfect for it with his long legs and big hands.

'So, yeah, I'm gutted—' I stopped. Amin was staring at me.

'What are you on about, mate? I'm talking about you and Rosie Linden. I heard you basically saved her life. You're a total legend.'

'That is not how it was,' I said, getting embarrassed. 'I just talked to her for a bit. I'm on about the Raptors. They dropped me. I'm never playing football again.'

'Does that mean I can finally get you to do triathlon?' He was laughing, actually laughing.

'Amin, you don't get it, do you? I was going to be a pro. My dreams are shattered.'

He shook his head, frowning.

'What?'

'You. That's what.' He squared up to me, his face close. 'Mate, I'm glad they dropped you. You've been no friend since they signed you up. You're never free to hang out and you've only got one thing to talk about. I think it's brilliant you're off the squad.'

It was the most spiteful thing anyone had ever said to me.

Over his shoulder I saw Imogen Richards in the distance. She smiled and waved, but I didn't wave back, I was too angry with Amin. How could he not get it?

At lunchtime, I caught up with Mr Harris in the corridor. Mr Harris is the head of PE and he runs the school football teams. I'm the captain of our year's team and I wanted everyone to know I wouldn't be playing any more and that I was done with football.

Mr Harris is a huge man. He used to play rugby for the county and wears shorts all year round. It doesn't matter where you stand on the school grounds, he can always be heard bellowing at someone to run faster, put more effort into it, or pass the ball. A lot of kids are terrified of him, but I like Mr Harris. If you love sport, he will go out of his way to help you.

'I heard about you not making the next stage of the squad, Jude, but it doesn't mean you should stop playing altogether. I know it's disappointing. Take some time to think about it, but don't stop. You're good.'

I shook my head. 'Not good enough, Mr Harris.'

'Just because you aren't good enough for the squad, doesn't mean you aren't good enough in other things. That's a negative message I would hate you to believe. You've got the physique, and natural sporting talent in spades.'

Kids spilled past in every direction, moving to the lunch hall and out to the Astroturf.

'You once told me that if I wanted something badly enough and worked hard, I could do anything.' I could feel my voice getting louder, the blood rushing to my face. 'I definitely wanted it badly enough and I certainly worked hard, so it's a lie, isn't it? I can't do anything I want. The whole lot. It's a lie.'

And I stormed off, leaving Mr Harris looking shocked and confused.

I was a total pain for the rest of that week. I was just so *angry*. I felt as though the football academy and Mr Harris had dangled a dream of being a professional footballer in front of me, only to snatch it away once I had devoted everything to it. Like they wanted to see how much I was prepared to sacrifice, knowing all along I wouldn't make it. It was Amin who told me the truth, like all good friends do in the end.

'Who told you that you were going to be a professional footballer, anyway?' he yelled at the end of school on Friday, as we stood by the gates. 'No one, that's who. Everyone says it's a long road through the academy to be a pro-player. Anything can happen, injuries, all sorts. No one said that because you got signed, you would make it, because no one *can* say that. *You* told yourself that, Jude. *You* built it up into this massive thing. And now you can't cope because it hasn't worked out. Get some perspective. You know someone whose life has fallen apart? Rosie Linden, that's who. My dad says there's no coming back from a mental problem like that.' He turned on his heel.

Deep down, I knew he was right about the football. But he was wrong about Rosie.

'That's not true,' I yelled. 'The paramedic said she's going to be fine. It will just take time.'

He kept walking.

I hadn't noticed Imogen at my elbow.

'She *is* going to be fine,' Imogen said, watching Amin with a fierce look on her face. She turned to me. 'I've been wanting to say thank you for being so kind to Rosie on Saturday. She's not been right for ages, messaging me in the middle of the night about lots of odd stuff. I didn't know what was wrong. I'm glad someone was there to help her.'

I didn't know what to say, because my cheeks were suddenly on fire, and I worried Imogen would notice, and it was weird finally speaking to her.

'I saw Rosie yesterday evening and she's loads better already. You should go and see her.'

When I still didn't say anything, she sighed and walked away. 'Have a nice weekend, Jude.'

As I watched her go, my cheeks finally cooling down, all I could think about was that stupid photo of us in the bath.

**11**

The weekend stretched before me like an eternity. Normally I would be at the academy in the mornings and spend the afternoons watching games or making up training schemes from online videos.

I couldn't bring myself to ring Amin and see what he was doing. He might be right, but I didn't want him to have the satisfaction of knowing it yet. I had nothing else to do. What if I did go and see Rosie?

On Saturday morning, I was in the kitchen and Mum was doing the washing-up.

'D'you think it would be weird if I went to see Rosie Linden?'

She looked at me over her shoulder. 'It will probably be a bit weird, but I don't think that's a reason not to go – it would be a kind thing to do. And if it's not a good time, at least she'll know people care about her.'

I wasn't really being kind. I had nothing else planned and the only person whose life seemed worse than mine at that moment was Rosie's. If I'm brutally honest, I thought it might make me feel better.

'I can drop you off on the way to the supermarket and pick you up on the way home?' Mum offered.

'All right then,' I said.

Mum hovered in the car while I rang the doorbell. Eddie answered the door. Maddy came up behind him, drying her hands on a tea towel. She looked tired.

'Jude, it's lovely to see you. What can I do for you?'

'I-I... um... wondered if Rosie is feeling up to visitors? Imogen said she came around the other evening.'

Maddy looked pleasantly surprised. 'Oh, that would be great. Come in.'

I waved to Mum, who honked the horn and drove off. In the kitchen, Rob had emptied a tin of nails and screws over the counter.

'Morning,' he said with a nod.

Eddie hopped around my feet.

'Are you Eddie?' I asked. 'I've seen your photo.'

He smiled shyly at me.

Maddy led me to the lounge.

'Rosie, sweetie. There's someone here to see you,' she said.

Rosie was sitting cross-legged on the sofa in her pyjamas and a hoody. When she saw me, she groaned and pulled her hood over her face.

'Maddy! I can't find it. It's not here,' called Rob from the kitchen.

'Hang on, Jude. I'll be back in one minute. Make yourself at home.'

I perched on the edge of the sofa. Rosie's hood was still pulled down firmly over her face.

I should never have come.

Eventually, she peeked out at me.

'Hi. I thought I'd come and see how you are.'

Imogen was right, Rosie looked loads better. Still pale and skinny as anything. The hoody looked massive on her. The orange stripy scarf she'd been wearing was draped across her lap, but someone must have washed it.

'Jude, I'm so embarrassed. I don't know what happened. Sometimes you were there on the bench next to me and then you'd be gone.'

I hadn't thought she might be embarrassed. 'Rosie, you were ill, really ill. That's nothing to be embarrassed about.' I actually scratched the top of my head like a confused cartoon character. 'That's like being embarrassed for getting run over in a car accident, or apologising for having the flu.'

She pushed back her hood. I was relieved to see her hair was clean and back to its bouncy self.

'I suppose you're right. I said some strange things, though. Mum says you had to come all the way here because I wouldn't let go of your hand.'

It was my turn to look embarrassed.

'Well, that was kind of my fault. My mum has this thing about hugs and oxytocin.' I shrugged. 'I thought it might help. It seemed to bring you back.'

She sat up. 'It did though, Jude. It did bring me back. Are you able to stay for longer or do you have to go?'

'My mum's going to pick me up when she's finished the shopping.' I moved onto the sofa next to her and we talked about some of the usual stuff going on at school.

After a few moments of silence, I said, 'Rosie, do you mind me asking, what did you think you were doing? When you said you were guarding us.'

She winced and shook her head. 'It's in fragments, like someone is switching a light on and off and I can only see the bits when the light is on. But, well…' She looked down at her hands and her voice dropped to a whisper. 'I thought I was a tiger and that I had to protect you all, like I was protecting my territory. I mean, what was I thinking?'

I didn't know what to say. I was ashamed of my hesitation because I wanted to reassure her, but I couldn't.

'The weirdest thing is that I still feel like it really happened. I remember actually feeling my body change into something else. I was so powerful. It feels so real in my head.'

'Were you like that the whole time you were missing? Thinking you were a tiger and protecting us? Did you sleep or eat?' I still couldn't understand how she survived.

'I don't remember exactly. I thought food wasn't

important. I just had to keep guarding, to keep you all safe.'

'Maybe the feeling it was real will fade as you get better?' I suggested.

Maddy popped her head around the door. 'Sorry about that. You okay in here? Would you like a drink, Jude?'

'Thanks, that would be great. Just water, please.'

When Maddy had gone, I tried again. 'You're looking much better already.'

Rosie smiled and shrugged. 'That's good, I suppose. I don't feel better exactly, but I do feel calmer. I'm taking pills which help. Not all the medication they could give me if I was older. Thirteen is quite young for this kind of thing to happen. I might grow out of it,' she said hopefully. 'There'll be assessments and I'll see a counsellor to learn how to manage my thoughts. It will take a while. The pills make me sleepy.'

'Oh, do you want me to go? Are you tired?'

'No, no, please stay. It's nice to see a different face. I've been looking through this.' She gestured to a cardboard box at her feet, filled with what looked like bric-a-brac. 'My gran died. The box was in her house with a label saying it was for me. This old scarf was in it.' She waved the end of the orange striped scarf at me.

'Here you are, Jude,' said Maddy, coming in with a glass of water. 'How are you feeling, Rosie? Okay?'

Rosie nodded wearily, as if she was getting asked that question a lot, and Maddy left us to it.

I took a sip of water, glancing at the box. I couldn't help thinking of what Alice had said about a family history of mental illness. How a mental illness could be passed down the generations. There was a lot of random stuff in that box.

'What else is in there?' I asked, peering in. Among antique-looking books, I could see an old loaf tin, jam jars labelled with old-fashioned handwriting and a well-used paint set.

'This was.' In Rosie's palm, she held an ammonite fossil, the size of a chocolate-chip cookie.

**12**

*London, December 1887*

'Emma, quickly.'

It was a week after Uncle Henry's visit, and Emma was shaken awake for a second time. Olivier looked down at her, face creased with worry.

'Olivier! What are you doing here? What's happened?'

'Please come. Don't make a sound.'

She wrapped herself in her dressing gown and hurried after him.

Huddled in the corner of the cold kitchen was her brother, his head hidden in his arms, the orange scarf looped around his shoulders.

'James.' She dropped to her knees at his side.

He raised his head as if it were as heavy as lead. It took a moment for him to focus on her.

'Emma,' he mumbled. Then his gaze slid from her face, eyes darting restlessly above her. She turned, half-expecting to see a cloud of insects swarming. His lips moved as if holding a silent conversation with an unseen person.

She shook him. 'James!'

He seemed unable to hear her voice or feel her touch. It was as though he were lost in another world. And he was filthy, fingernails dark with dirt. *What was wrong?* Leaning forward, she felt his brow, but there was no fever or chill.

How had Olivier got him here from Oxford and into the house without alarming anyone? He looked worn out, his sleeves rolled up, waistcoat undone.

'What's happened, Olivier?'

He shook his head helplessly. 'Emma, can't you see? He's ill. It's his mind that's sick.'

'I-I don't understand...'

'The first time was when we were at St Scabrous, the term after that wonderful summer we spent at Kersbrook.' Olivier's voice was hushed, but he spoke rapidly, eyes pleading with her to grasp the situation.

'Thankfully, he recovered. James and I read all we could, and I was fortunate to attend a lecture by Dr Emil Kraepelin when he visited Oxford, discussing just such a condition as James's. It's a biological malfunction – possible to recover from, though prone to relapse. We worked hard together to prevent him falling ill again. But your father's sudden passing and your Uncle Henry's plans must have been more than he could stand.'

'No, that's not right, Olivier.' Emma shook her head. 'It's me. I'm the one who's ill. Not him!'

Olivier regarded her sadly. 'James knew there was never anything wrong with you that couldn't be explained by a nasty bump on the head. But your father was convinced of it. Fits or seizures are often seen as a symptom of mental disturbance and this sickness ran in your mother's family. It's not such a leap to see how he believed you inherited the same affliction. And shame is a powerful force.' He sighed. 'It was clear, even to James, that your father was deeply ashamed of your mother's illness. He expected madness to erupt in you at any moment, and watched you like a hawk. Any sign of emotion became evidence to support his theory.'

Mrs Carter's conversation with the new cook replayed in Emma's mind.

*'She is afflicted with a malady of the mind which comes from her mother's side.'*

Mother's stay in an asylum, her own confinement, the household's fear of her, creeping around the house with no ill-effects... She knew Olivier was right.

'James despaired of your father's treatment of you, then started to experience his own difficulties. He thought he could control it...' His voice trailed away.

She studied him, hot tears brimming. 'It should never have been me kept away in the attic. He was the one who needed protecting.' A stab of anger flashed in her chest. 'What a waste!'

She turned to her poor, broken brother, burying her face in the crumpled handkerchief Olivier offered. He kneeled down and put his arm around her.

'But he has been safe, don't you see? His greatest fear was being locked away. I'm certain that's why he insisted on going to Bethlem that time, as though it were a fate he had to stare straight in the eye to give him strength to fight on. And he has remained free and well until now, hasn't he? He can be well again. You must believe it.'

She grasped Olivier's hand. 'In most part, thanks

to you by the sounds of it—' She jumped to her feet. 'But if they find him like this, they *will* lock him away!'

'Yes,' replied Olivier, getting to his feet too. 'And there's more. If James is admitted to an asylum, his inheritance will pass to your uncle. Both of you will be reliant on his generosity and subject to the choices he thinks best.'

'He cannot do that to us!' She stared at him, realising for the first time how deeply her fate was entwined with her brother's and how little power she had. 'What can I do?'

'Emma, I have a plan, but it's a bold one and I need your help. Will you hear me out?'

She nodded, frantic for any glimmer of hope.

Olivier glanced at his watch. 'The last train to Devon from Paddington leaves in one hour. I have booked us a first-class compartment.' He slipped his hand into his pocket and held out a brass key. 'We're going to Kersbrook, Emma. Tonight! It's the only place where he stands a chance of getting well.'

Immediately, she could imagine them there, even in the depths of winter. Olivier was right. James would be well again at Kersbrook.

'But what about Uncle Henry? He will never allow it. How will we move James? And what about your studies?' Questions tumbled out.

Olivier put a hand on James's shoulder. 'He can walk if he leans on me. I've given him medication that calms him. I'll write to your uncle once we are safely in Devon. He'll be more than glad to make up a socially acceptable reason why the two of you should remain at Kersbrook and still receive a living from the business. James's illness would cause a scandal for the family were it to become public. Your uncle will do anything to avoid that. As for me—' His grim expression softened. 'I'll return to Oxford after Christmas to finish my studies and then, dear Emma, the success of the plan is down to you.'

She looked at her brother. 'I can do it.'

He nodded. 'Very well, but we *must* hurry. If any of the servants find him here like this…' He didn't need to finish the sentence.

Creeping back through the house, Emma suppressed a gasp at the sight of Timothy, bleary-eyed and half-asleep, standing in the corridor with a candle. She stepped quickly into a doorway.

He stood still, muttering. 'Sure I heard a noise. Those blasted pigeons. This house gives me the creeps at night. Be seeing the ghost of the old master next.'

Emma almost collapsed with relief as he blundered off to bed. She fled upstairs to her room.

In the darkness, she fumbled for her clothes, dressing quickly. She could hardly think what to pack in her bag. Hairbrush. Nightcap. Shawl. What else? Scanning the shadows, Emma's eyes fell on her mother's desk. To leave it behind... She stroked the smooth wood. After all those years spent sitting at it, huddled over her microscope, making detailed drawings and daydreaming of setting sail on imaginary expeditions. It was like leaving a part of herself behind. But it was time to say goodbye. She rummaged through a pile of books, toppling a second pile in her haste. She halted.

But the house was silent. She picked up the book she'd been looking for, her favourite, about Mary Anning, and placed it on the desk so it was square with the corner. Feeling in her pocket, she brought out her ammonite fossil, laying it on top of the book.

'When he is well, I'll come back for you,' she promised under her breath.

One last, long look. Then she flicked shut the clasp on her bag and ran from the room.

The light from the streetlamps reflected off the wet cobbles as the carriage rattled through the streets on the way to the station.

At Paddington, the stationmaster raised an eyebrow at James's huddled figure leaning on Olivier's shoulder. 'Is he fit enough to be travelling?'

Olivier was like lightning with his response. 'He has a terrible chest infection. Doctors recommend sea air.'

Emma nodded in support.

'Funny time to be travelling with an invalid,' said the man, looking at his pocket watch.

'The doctors don't believe it is contagious, but we can't be completely sure,' Emma blurted out.

That's what they had thought about her. She knew now this couldn't be true.

The stationmaster's eyes widened. 'Indeed?' He took a step backwards, pulling a handkerchief from his pocket, covering his mouth and nose. 'Wise to have booked this compartment out, then. Don't want anything catching.' His voice was muffled behind the cloth as he slammed the door shut.

Emma sank down in her seat, unable to relax. At last, the train chugged away from the platform. She watched the lights of London slide past until they were replaced by dark countryside.

**13**

Emma watched James's reflection in the window. He was sleeping, curled up in a ball beneath a blanket. But there was nothing restful about this journey.

Olivier had telegrammed Dillis – who had the farm at Kersbrook with her husband Harold – to tell her they were coming and to get the house ready. Emma wondered how much she knew of James's condition.

During those long summers in Devon, Dillis had cooked and cleaned for the family. James and Emma had known her their whole lives. She'd wiped their chins, bandaged cut knees and slipped them slabs of her famous lardy cake from the day they could toddle from their nurse's lap.

But oh, how Dillis loved James! He was her favourite and she made no pains to hide it. There was always a crisp, green apple for him in her pocket, or an extra slice of cake. As the lights of towns and villages blinked past in the darkness, Emma worried whether Dillis would be the stumbling block in their plan. Emma was the invalid, the delicate one. How would Dillis react when she saw her beloved James in such a state? Would she call the doctor and demand he be admitted to the asylum?

She met them at the station with the cart and pony. Without a word, she took James's arm and gently but firmly guided him along the platform. Wise, wonderful Dillis had read between the lines and Emma saw tears welling in her eyes at the sight of her favourite boy.

James sat hunched in the back of the cart, hat pulled down and collar up, the striped, orange scarf wrapped around his face so only his eyes could be seen. As Emma watched Dillis heap kisses on his forehead, she wasn't sure he even recognised her.

'Er, James is—' Olivier began.

'Shush, don't say another word. I see how it is. You brought him to the best place. If he can get well anywhere, it's here. Fresh air and home cooking is what he needs.' Dillis turned to Emma as she took the reins. 'Between me and Miss Emma, we'll get him right, won't we, my lover?'

The pony set off at a jog. In the cart, side by side with her brother, Emma reached into her pocket for her ammonite, before remembering she'd left it behind. James sighed heavily. They had made it this far. Emma tucked her hand into the crook of his arm. She knew that here she could be strong.

They arrived at the house in the frosty darkness, their breath making clouds in the air. When Emma saw the porch of Kersbrook in the lamplight, it was as if a great weight lifted from her. Olivier squeezed the front door key into her palm as he helped her from the cart.

At Kersbrook, all would be well.

*Devon, Summer Term 2023*

I turned over the ammonite in my hand, before passing it back to Rosie. It was heavier than I expected.

'This reminds me of one of those games where you have to guess the connection,' I said, only

half-joking. I picked up an antique-looking book, *The Life of Mary Anning.*

'Oh, don't.' Rosie placed the fossil next to her on the sofa and fiddled with the catch of a leather jewellery case she'd dug out of the box. 'I'm already feeling like there's some hidden message my gran's expecting me to decipher and I'm too dozy to work it out. Here, see if you can open this—'

With a twist, the catch flipped open under my thumb. Inside, a delicate silver chain and pendant sparkled against blue velvet. There was a long silence while Rosie stared at it.

'Prodromal symptoms,' she said at last.

'What?'

'Weird behaviour, prodromal symptoms, that's what they're called. The crisis nurse talked about them. Like mild symptoms of psychosis that lead up to the full-blown thing.'

'Oh, right.' I was learning a lot about mental health these days, but I had no clue what that had to do with the necklace.

'My gran always wore this necklace. The pendant's Saint Blaise, the patron saint of wild animals.' Rosie bit her lip. 'She knew it was coming, I reckon. She

99

recognised the symptoms. She found me once, maybe a year and a half ago, sitting on the rail of the bannisters on the upstairs landing with my feet dangling down. I've no idea how I got there. I remember thinking it would be a good place to leap from, but where to, I'm not sure. I'd been having trouble sleeping and I don't think I'd brushed my hair or cleaned my teeth for days. It wasn't important. Sometimes things felt so unreal, like I was floating through the world, looking at it, but not really a part of it.'

'What did she do?'

'Who?'

'Your gran. When she found you sitting on the bannister?'

'Oh, she freaked out. She pulled me back and kneeled on the floor with me. I remember staring at the pendant in the crook of her neck and feeling quite calm, wondering why she was so upset. She made me promise not to tell anyone. I don't think she knew that if she'd told a doctor, they could have prevented it getting so serious.'

Rosie paused. 'But things were different in the past, so I don't blame her. You had to keep quiet or you'd end up in a lunatic asylum.'

Outside, a car horn beeped. Mum.

'I've got to go,' I said, putting down the book.

I desperately wanted to say something that might help, but my mind was a blank. She looked so sad as I left her. She'd picked up the ammonite fossil, turning it over in her hands. What I wished I'd said was how I hadn't wanted to leave, and how it had been nice, sitting there, talking with her.

**14**

I couldn't stop thinking about Rosie and her gran.
I couldn't stop thinking about Amin either. Amin
would jump into a freezing lake if he thought I was
drowning, that's how good a friend he is. And I'd
do the same for him. I felt bad for the way I'd yelled
and decided I would apologise as soon as I saw him
on Monday.

'Mate, no worries. Gone. Forgotten.' He gave me
one of his hugs, which is more like being bashed
in the chest and slapped on the back at the same
time. I don't think you get much oxytocin from one
of Amin's hugs, but I was glad of it anyway. I was
careful to avoid seeing Mr Harris. I wasn't ready to
say sorry to him yet.

At the end of the day, I stood at the school
gates wondering what to do. Everyone else had

left already, everyone except Zak Riley, who was leaning against the railings looking at his phone. Unusually, he was on his own.

Standing there was another reminder – as if I needed it – of how my life had suddenly changed. Normally on a Monday I would have gone straight to football academy after school. This was causing a load of stress for Mum, though she was trying not to show it. Mum couldn't swap her shifts at such short notice, so she'd signed me up for the dodgeball, Ultimate Frisbee and basketball after-school clubs. There was no way I was going to any of them. I was off sport for good.

All day I'd been toying with the idea of going to see Rosie, but I couldn't make up my mind. What if she didn't want to see me? I probably should have told Mum straight, but she has enough to worry about. If I'd told her I was going to Rosie's instead of dodgeball, she'd make a thing of trying to arrange it with Maddy. It all felt too complicated.

'Hey, Simmons.' Zak looked up from his phone. 'Got nowhere to go, now you've been kicked out of football academy? Loser.'

I clenched my jaw.

I've never heard Zak say anything nice to anyone. Besides, he was wrong. I did have somewhere to go – Rosie's. I tried not to think about what I'd do if she didn't want to see me. Getting kicked out of the academy was like being dumped overboard, my whole purpose slipping over the horizon with the current. Chatting with Rosie, it didn't seem quite so bad. I set off in the direction of her house. But I had to pass Zak first.

'You don't live that way, Simple Simmons. Too simple to know where your house is? That why they kicked you off the squad? Didn't know which way to kick the ball? You're just too thick.'

I gritted my teeth. Zak has a sixth sense for your weak spot. Ask anyone in my year – almost everyone's been on the receiving end at some point. He zones in, chipping away.

'Wait a minute, I get it.' He stood up now, sniggering. 'That's the way to Rosie Linden's. I heard what happened – you're her knight in shining armour. Is she your new girlfriend? That's a match made in heaven. Simple Simmons and his wacko girlfriend, Loony Linden. Off her head, that one. Off. Her. Head!' He shouted the last bit. But I wasn't going to give him the satisfaction of replying. Attention is like oxygen to a bog brush like Zak. I hunched my shoulders and carried on down the street, but inside I was raging. Is that what everyone thought about me and Rosie? Couldn't they see she was ill? As soon as I was round the corner, I sprinted the rest of the way, pounding my irritation out through each step.

Maddy answered the door. 'Hello, Jude. Back so soon? Well, that's nice. Come in.' She still looked tired, but less so today.

Eddie was watching cartoons in the lounge. He came running over. 'Hi, Jude. Will you kick a ball with me? Rosie says you're in the football academy.'

'He's here to see Rosie,' said Maddy, ruffling Eddie's hair.

'Maybe another time, Eddie?' I said. Great – I was even going to be a failure to a six-year-old once he knew I'd been dropped.

'She's up in her room,' said Maddy, nodding towards the stairs.

I knocked before opening Rosie's door. She was sitting on her bed, back to the wall, staring into the middle distance. The box with her gran's stuff was beside her and she was holding a white envelope in her hands. For a moment I panicked, thinking she'd gone again. But she shook her head and smiled at me. She must have been daydreaming.

'Jude, hi. Look at this.' She held up the envelope and tipped a big, old-fashioned brass key with an ornate loop at the top into her hand. 'It's one of my gran's things from that box. Wouldn't it be cool to find which lock it fits? I wouldn't even know where to start looking. Anyway, how are you?' She frowned. 'Hey, isn't Monday a Raptors night? Don't tell me you're skipping it? Ben Reid, over the road, is on the squad and he's never at home. Everyone knows it's 100 per cent commitment or you're out.'

I tried to laugh off her teasing, but I obviously didn't do a very good job.

'What's wrong, Jude?'

'Can I sit down?'

'Yeah, course.'

She shuffled over on the bed and I sat, resting my elbows on my knees.

'I didn't get selected to move on to the next stage of the squad. I'm out of the Raptors, Rosie.'

'I don't understand. I heard you were really good.'

I shook my head. 'Not good enough.'

And then it came pouring out – how my hopes for the future were ruined, and what on earth was I going to do now?

'I'm really sorry, Jude. After all that training too. I know how you guys on the squad spend half your lives at the club.'

She stopped, a look flashing across her face, and I realised she'd seen through me. She knew I wasn't visiting her just to be kind, but because I didn't have anywhere else to go. In a strange way, I was glad – it made us equals, both a bit lost.

She shook her head. 'If it makes you feel any better, it's reassuring that someone else's life isn't going to plan.'

'You've got plans?' I asked without thinking, as if I was the only one.

Rosie sighed and leaned back. 'I wanted to be an environmental campaigner. To travel the world, helping protect wildlife and nature.' She gazed at her posters.

'What's stopping you?'

She tapped her temple. 'This. Can you imagine what would happen to someone like me if I went off into the middle of a jungle or up a mountain? And have you seen the state of my mum? Imagine what she'd be like if I got sick in some far-off place.'

'But you'll get past this and you'll be fine. The nurses and doctors must have told you the same thing. You're getting proper help now. We don't live in the Victorian times with asylums and straitjackets.' I looked at her posters, waving at the tiger. 'I'll sound stupid saying this, and I know the tiger thing was a hallucination or delusion or whatever, but you remind me of a tiger. No, don't tell me to shut up—'

It had just occurred to me, but I was sure I was right. Mum reckons you find out what people are really made of when they're up against it.

'I mean, on the inside... All right, I've never actually *met* a tiger, but they're supposed to be strong and brave and protective, right? Like you. Even when you were seriously ill, you were looking out for people. That says something about you, Rosie. Lots of people get mentally ill and they

108

get better.' I so wanted her to understand that I absolutely believed she would be okay.

She was quiet. I thought I'd gone too far with my little pep talk. Then she said, 'Yes, lots of people do, but there's no promises.'

I thought she was going to cry. I'm not very good when people cry, so I quickly changed the subject. 'So... who's your favourite Premier League manager?'

'All right, now my turn,' Rosie said, half an hour later. 'Wedges or curly fries?'

'Easy, curly fries.'

'Ketchup or mayo?'

'Oooh, tricky. Both?' We had covered a lot of ground since my football manager question. I now knew a lot of random stuff about Rosie, like... she's vegetarian (no surprise there), her one essential for Christmas is paper chains made out of newspaper (family tradition, apparently) and she would invite Aretha Franklin to tea over Elvis (no contest).

I glanced down at my watch. I needed to go. Rosie looked at me.

'How many nights a week did you do the Raptors?'

'Three. Monday, Wednesday and Friday, and then Saturday and Sunday mornings.'

'So, I'll see you on Wednesday then, will I?'

I gave her a sheepish smile. 'Yeah,' I said. 'If that's all right?'

She nodded. 'It's all right.'

*Kersbrook, 19 December 1887 – 4 January 1888*

Emma searched the back room her father used as a study, pulling open the drawers in his desk. It was the morning after their flight from London and old newspapers would be perfect for what she had in mind. The drawers were empty, except for one which was locked. It was old and worn so that the drawer came open a little way, then stuck. She squinted inside. What papers would Father keep here at Kersbrook? Where might the key be?

'*Emma.*' Her father's voice seemed to cross time, transporting her to his study in London, clutching James's letter. '*What are you doing here? Turn around and answer me.*'

With a shudder, she shoved the drawer shut and, spotting a pile of dusty newspapers on a

shelf, grabbed them and hurried out of the room. Whatever was in that drawer, she would leave it well alone.

She kneeled down on the rug in the conservatory and began tearing the newspapers into strips for paper chains. Anxiety about whether Uncle Henry would agree to Olivier's plan niggled at her.

'Can I help you, Em?'

She looked up, startled. She had heard James pacing the house all night. His voice was hoarse and his eyes were weary, but there was something of his old self about him. It was enough for her to know that Kersbrook was already working its magic.

Christmas should have been a bleak and dismal one after all that had happened, but it was far from that. Though James still spent most of his days huddled in the corner, beyond exhausted, Emma always remembered it as one of the most perfect Christmases. Olivier helped her hang the paper chains and, encouraged by Emma, James added more of his own. Christmas Day came crisp and cold, the sky bright blue, and beyond the conservatory windows, the ground sparkled thick with frost. They had never been at Kersbrook in the

winter and everything was still and peaceful. Only Olivier ventured out for more coal. Inside, they played card games and chess by the fire.

Never having cooked for themselves before, they weren't up to preparing Christmas dinner, and lunch around the huge table with the Kerrs' extended family was too big a risk. Instead, they ate cold chicken and redcurrant jelly sandwiches, followed by mince pies that Olivier had cycled to get from the bakers.

As the night drew in on Christmas Day, Emma lit the lamps, shielding the glowing taper from the draughts. James sat back in his chair, gazing out of the window.

'I always said this house was perfect,' he said.

Emma looked over at him. His face was calm.

'But imagine a whole belt of trees planted around it. Kersbrook would be like an enchanted house, deep in the woods. What do you think, Em?'

Olivier and Emma exchanged a glance. It was the most James had said since they'd arrived. Was he preparing himself never to be fully well, living in a hidden house far from prying eyes? If only Uncle Henry would agree for them to stay.

Olivier stood by James's chair, looking out over the garden. 'You're right, James. A tree-planting scheme would improve Kersbrook greatly. You should compile a list of the most suitable species and we'll begin in the spring.'

Dillis arrived early on Boxing Day with a sack of flour under one arm and a packet of fresh yeast in the other.

'Mister James!' she called, without stopping on her way to the kitchen. 'I am wanting you.'

James frowned and sighed, but got up and went after her. Emma and Olivier couldn't resist following. What was she up to?

'Now, I don't have long. I've got to get the Boxing Day ham in, so heed me well,' she said, her thick hands fisted on her even thicker hips. There was no arguing with her.

'Running a household when you're accustomed to servants will take some getting used to. It's very well me looking after you each summer, but I can't year round. I'm going to instruct you in the proper

way of doing things. Mister James, you will be in charge of the bread. Stoke up the oven. We want it nice and hot. Then wash your hands.'

James didn't answer. His face was blank, but after a few seconds he went to the sink and began rolling up his shirtsleeves.

Dillis bustled into the pantry in search of salt, muttering, 'It's as though that cold fish of an uncle wants them to starve.'

Olivier shrugged at Emma, who grinned, and they sat down at the kitchen table to watch.

Dillis's baking and cooking had always seemed a kind of alchemy to Emma, turning basic ingredients into mouth-watering feasts. Her skills were even more miraculous given Emma's ignorance of the kitchen at Old Brompton Road. Her plain diet had inspired no such devotion. Since returning to Kersbrook, they had survived on fruit, pies from the bakery and hard-boiled eggs. Dillis's arrival was timely.

'Now,' Dillis said, tying an apron around James's waist. 'Begin like this with flour and add salt.' She showed him how to mix yeast with warm water and sugar. He didn't speak, concentrating

on running his fingers through the beige liquid until it dissolved.

'There's nothing better than your own two hands for mixing bread, so get on in there,' Dillis told him, tipping the bubbling yeast into the flour, and thrusting the bowl at James. He began so timidly that she took the bowl, expertly scraping the edges of it with her hand to fold every bit of flour into the mixture.

'Like that,' she said, passing it back.

He frowned, then followed her example. The dough rose quickly in the warm kitchen and Dillis used the lull in proceedings to show Emma how to make a simple vegetable soup.

When she was satisfied with the dough, Dillis dusted the scrubbed tabletop with flour and tipped it out. Emma paused, mid-stir, to watch her knead it, deftly turning it with her left hand and pushing down with the palm of her right.

'Your turn.'

James began slowly, building up to a steady rhythm. Round and round went the dough.

'Now, roll it like this into a loaf.' Dillis demonstrated, handing it back for him to try.

He rolled it over, letting it drop into the tin, then looked up and smiled. To Emma, it was like water after days in the desert.

Dillis wiped her hands and undid her apron. 'That flour will last you a week. Then it will be your job, Mister James, to walk over to the mill for more. The miller will give you yeast as well.'

After explaining when to take the bread out of the oven and how to tell it was done by tapping on the bottom of the loaf, Dillis went on her way.

'You know where I am if you need me,' she said briskly.

Emma followed her to the door. 'You're so kind,' she said.

Dillis took Emma's hand in hers. 'Breaks my heart to see him like this, Miss Emma, but there aren't many problems that can't be kneaded out on a bread board.' She turned with a cheery wave, calling over her shoulder, 'I'll bring seed potatoes for chitting tomorrow, and teach him pastry next. We'll make rabbit pie lovers of you yet!'

Emma laughed and went inside to the kitchen, where the smell of baking bread and hot soup was already filling the room.

Olivier caught the 12.30 train to Paddington on the 4th of January. Emma walked with him through the lanes to the station, hardly able to put one foot in front of the other. She was full of trepidation. Would it be like that awful trip to Bethlem, where all she could do was stand by, no use to either of them?

'I'll return at Easter,' Olivier said, one hand on the open carriage door. 'But in the meantime, please write and tell me how you both go.'

'Of course. Thank you, Olivier, for everything you've done for us.'

He gave her a sad smile and squeezed her shoulder. 'He would've done the same for me.'

The train pulled away in a cloud of steam, leaving Emma alone on the platform.

Suddenly, the sky seemed to spin – altogether too wide and too big, thoughts drumming on the inside of her skull.

Alone.

Outside.

The future full of doubt.

Panic exploded inside her. She stumbled to her knees, gasping, eyes squeezed tight.

'Are you all right, missy?'

The stationmaster peered at her with concern. She made herself breathe. In. Out. In. Out.

Trying to keep the quiver from her voice, she answered, 'Quite all right, thank you. Just a trip.'

She forced herself to her feet, though she wasn't certain they would hold her.

'Well now, you take more care.'

'I will.' As she walked away, legs like jelly and heart pounding, she became aware of the warmth of the winter sun, soft like a stroke. She knew the sensation was caused by light waves, radiation falling on the electrons in her skin. But it felt as if the universe were smiling – hardly a rational thought! She turned her face upwards, taking a deep breath, relishing the feeling of her ribcage expanding.

Here she was, outside, alone. Slowly, she smiled too.

She felt her life stretch ahead of her. Not hiding in an attic, but free in the open air. And James would be well.

She ran back to the house with wings on her heels, her heart full with the joy of being alive.

**20**

*Devon, Summer Term 2023*

I couldn't believe it when I saw Mum's car parked outside our house. I'd left Rosie's in plenty of time. What was she doing home so early? I should have guessed that Mr Harris would have called her when I didn't show at dodgeball. I found her sitting at the kitchen table.

'Jude! Where have you been? Mr Harris reassured me you would turn up, but I've been worried sick.' She looked it too.

'I went to Rosie's.'

She stared at me. 'Why didn't you tell me?'

I shrugged. 'You were so worried about your shifts and what you were going to do with me. It was too difficult to explain that I didn't want to go to dodgeball, or Ultimate Frisbee, or any of those things. And anyway, I wasn't even sure I was going to Rosie's until the end of school.'

Mum sighed. 'I'm sorry. This is my fault. I should have given more thought to what you wanted to do. But I didn't like the idea of you being on your own.'

'It's not your fault, honest.'

'Are you all right? You had your heart set on football academy. You'd worked so hard and put me to shame with all your training! I keep meaning to get back to netball…' She shook her head. 'It must be such a disappointment.'

I sat down at the table opposite. 'It still feels pretty rubbish, but I'll be fine. It's actually quite nice going over to Rosie's. She said I can go on Wednesday. Is that okay?'

Mum took my hands in hers and smiled. 'Yes, that's okay.' Her gaze drifted thoughtfully. I knew this look well, it was my mum getting an idea. She planted her palms on the table and stood up.

'Now, I don't know why I didn't think of it before, but I'm going to bake Rosie's family a cake. It can be tough in those early weeks, getting over something like this. It's hard on the family.' She paused. 'I'll bake one for Walter while I'm at it.'

That's my mum, interfering: if in doubt, hug people or feed them better.

'Mum, what's that?' There was something different about the kitchen dresser.

'What?' she asked, glancing around. 'Oh, this?' She pointed to a framed photograph. 'I found it stuffed down the back of the TV cabinet. I can't think how it got there. You were all so cute and I had a spare frame. I told Jackie about it and she's asked for a copy. Happy memories.'

Jackie is Imogen's mum. Mum had only gone and found the naked bath photo, framed it, and put it in the kitchen so I could be re-shamed every time I ate my cornflakes. There was no way I was having Amin in the house while that was there, he'd never let me forget it.

When I arrived at Rosie's with the cake on Wednesday, Maddy thanked me and showed me through to the kitchen. Rosie was sitting on the back step of their house, looking out over the garden. I wish me and Mum had a garden like Rosie's. Ours is more of a courtyard. There's a bit of grass, but it's mostly worn away from where I've played football. Rosie's garden is long, with big trees and shrubs making it feel like there are no other houses around. On that afternoon, sunlight flickering over the grass, Rosie reminded me of a sunbathing cat. Her eyes were closed, and she was clearly enjoying the warmth on her face. The old book of her gran's about Mary Anning lay open in her lap. Eddie was kicking a football, taking sucks from an ice lolly in a long plastic wrapper.

'Jude!' he cried when he saw me. 'Come and play.'

'Hey,' Rosie called, then to her brother, 'I don't think Jude's up for football right now, Eddie.'

'It's okay,' I told her. I went and crouched beside him. 'Eddie, I got dropped by the Raptors.'

'Oh.' He looked at me, then scowled. 'Football's rubbish anyway.' He kicked the ball hard, down the garden. 'Can you shoot hoops? I've got a basketball, but I'm not very good.'

I grinned. 'Basketball, cool.'

There was a hoop and net bolted to the wall. I kicked up the basketball into my hands, dodging around him as I bounced it, making him laugh.

Then, stretch, shoot, BOOM! *He scooores!* I raised my hand for a high-five and Eddie erupted into giggles. We played for a while, me doing my best impression of an NBA commentator. It was fun.

'All right, enough now, Eddie,' said Rosie. 'I want my friend back.'

His shoulders sagged. 'He's my friend too.'

Rosie laughed. 'All right, let's agree to share him. Can I have my turn now?'

Eddie sighed and nodded, but he looked happy enough as he went to look for his football. I sat down next to Rosie.

'So, how's it going?'

She looked at me out of one eye, the other closed to the sun. 'Good, actually. I had my first session of counselling today. I was going to have to wait for ages, but a space came up.'

'That's great.'

'And look at this.' She held up the book. Written in faded brown ink on the inside cover was a name:

Emma Linden
51° 29' 56.04" N
0° 09' 54.00" E

'Woah, a long-lost relative?' I asked. 'Are those coordinates?'

'Looks like it. We know nothing about Gran's side of the family. Remember when Mrs Elliot had us find out what our relatives did in World War Two?'

I nodded. Turned out my great-grandad spent the war driving a tractor in Cyprus. Not exactly exciting.

'I never thought till now, but Gran only talked about Grandad's side of the family. Why be so secretive?'

I studied Rosie's face, trying to stop a niggly worry from making me frown. People are only secretive when they've got something to hide. What was hidden in Rosie's family history?

But Rosie met my gaze, eyes shining. 'I'd like to try and find out. Mum says she knows nothing. Whoever Emma was, she must have loved this book. It's so well-read. I'm not surprised, it's great. Do you know anything about Mary Anning?'

I shrugged. 'Only that she lived up the coast and dug for fossils.'

'Same as me, then,' Rosie admitted. 'But she's actually amazing. She survived being struck by lightning when she was a baby and her dog was buried under a landslide when she was collecting fossils and,' her voice was getting faster with her excitement, 'and, and… she *literally* revolutionised science!'

We both laughed. It was good sitting there together in the open air with the sun smiling down on us.

*Kersbrook, January 1888*

Two or three days after Olivier returned to Oxford, the clattering of cartwheels could be heard in the lane, followed by a loud rapping at the door.

'Delivery for Miss Emma Linden,' called a man's voice.

Two men outside tipped their caps at Emma. 'Where do you want these, miss?' The first man indicated three wooden crates.

'Oh, through here, I think. Do you know what's inside or who sent them?'

'There's a note, miss,' said the man, edging the first crate to the side of the cart so they could lift it down.

Olivier's handwriting! At last, some news. She had been waiting anxiously to hear of his meeting with Uncle Henry. She peeled open the envelope.

*Dear Emma,*

*Your uncle has agreed to our plan! You'll both be provided for from your father's shares in the businesses. These will remain in James's name, but most importantly, you'll be left in peace at Kersbrook.*

*He suggests your Old Brompton Road home is sold, as you'll have no more use for it. He'll put the proceeds towards your keep. I felt sure you would agree to this.*

*He was oddly difficult to pin down about Kersbrook. He mentioned wanting to sell it, but some legal grey area in your father's will prevented him from doing so. I had a strange sense that he holds a grudge against the house. The main thing is that he assured me you can both go on living there as long as you wish, and I believe he is a man of his word.*

*You can thank Mrs Carter for the enclosed. She packed it up at my request. I hope it will*

*help you feel at home. She is a better woman
than I gave her credit for. She asked me to
wish you all the very best.*

*I will write soon, Emma.*

*Olivier*

Emma's hands trembled. It was settled, then. Kersbrook would be their home for as long as they needed it. But they still needed to be careful to keep James's illness a secret or it might not stay that way.

James appeared, blinking, in the conservatory, where the men had manoeuvred the crates.

'Have you got what you need to open the boxes, sir?' asked one of the men.

'Er, yes, there are tools in one of the outbuildings,' Emma said quickly.

James bade a hasty retreat to find them.

'Will that be all, miss?'

'Yes, thank you,' Emma said, tipping the men and closing the door behind them. She had done it! She'd acted as if she took receipt of unexpected deliveries every day of the week.

In the conservatory, James had already cracked open one of the crates.

'It's Mother's desk!' He heaved it up and away from the rest of the packaging. 'Let's put it here on the rug, Em. You can draw and read looking out over the garden. Where's the chair?'

She stepped aside as he pounced on the second crate. 'They sent your books and drawings too! Look, here is your book on Mary Anning and your old ammonite!'

She was delighted to have her precious belongings, but Emma couldn't help laughing at her brother's enthusiasm. He ran his hand across the desktop.

'I wish we could have known her,' he said suddenly. 'Or at least, known what happened.' He shook his head. 'It might have helped, that's all.'

Emma felt uncomfortable. She had never shown him the message carved into the desk. It had always felt like a promise just for her. But now that seemed childish. They both needed that promise.

'Come and look at this.' Emma crouched down. 'You'll think me foolish, but it makes me feel she's here with us.'

James kneeled beside her. 'What is it?'

He ran his fingers over the words.

*I will keep you safe.*

Emma thought of the locked drawer in her father's desk. Might there be something inside about their mother? And a way to break the lock? Her gaze slid to the tools James had used to open the crates. What would Father say if he could read her thoughts now?

# 17

The wind caught at their coats and pulled at Emma's skirts as they set off the next day. James stopped at the gate that opened onto the Kerrs' fields. His skin was pale and clammy, lips moving in silent, intense discussion. His eyes shot upwards. Emma thought his attention was caught by a bird breaking cover and flying low overhead, but there was nothing.

Frightened, she took his hand in hers. The change in him had been quick. Clearly, he wasn't better. He was working hard all the time, his mind half here, half in another world.

'We don't have to go.'

He stared, as if unable to understand what she was saying. Then, to her relief, he nodded and, keeping hold of her hand, carefully placed one foot in front of the other.

Progress was slow but steady. The way to the mill

was along muddy footpaths across the fields and Emma was glad of her leather boots. At the mill, James swung like a pendulum away from his withdrawn mood. He came alive with curiosity at the sight of the two great wheels hanging side by side in the mill leat, questioning the miller about the mechanisms, barely letting him finish before moving on to his next question, and gesticulating wildly. Emma wasn't sure whether to feel reassured, but the miller seemed delighted by James's interest. He weighed out a bag of flour and happily showed them how the river flowed fast and strong, powering the wheels, water dripping from the wooden slats as they turned. By the time they left, the light was fading and before Emma knew it, they were on an unfamiliar path winding up into woodland then petering out altogether.

'We've gone wrong, James. Let's retrace our steps.' She glanced around anxiously.

'We can't be far from home. If we loop through these woods, we should come out at the end of our lane.' He strode on under the trees.

She hesitated. 'Please, James. I'd rather take the path we know. It's getting dark and we could become even more lost.'

'It's a shortcut, Em. Come on!'

She had no choice but to hurry after him, boots slipping and sliding on the muddy ground.

'Halt! Trespassers!' A sharp voice barked through the shadows. They froze.

'This is private property!'

A tall man in a flat cap and tweed jacket marched towards them. At his side were three large dogs, teeth bared and snarling. His face was a hard mask, stencilled with a precise moustache. Cradled over his arm, a rifle. Emma peered through the gloom. There was something oddly familiar about him.

'Can you not understand English?' The man raised the gun to his eye, levelling the end of the barrel at James.

'Please! We had no idea... we're lost...' Emma was shrill with fear.

James's expression was unreadable. Emma felt tension radiating from him.

'Want to test me? I will shoot.' There was a nasty glint in the man's eye, as if he might enjoy the opportunity. 'I was at the Siege of Lucknow in India. I know how to deal with riff-raff. Even killed a tiger out there. I've shot and trapped more vermin than you've had hot dinners. Now clear off!' His snarl rose to a shout, the dogs letting out a volley of barks.

'No!' Emma screamed, terrified. 'We're lost!'

'You're not lost. I know who you are. You live in *my* house. Get out of here!'

James turned on his heel. He stalked past Emma, striding away without waiting for her to follow. It was all she could do to run to keep him in sight, over the fields in the dim light, and along the muddy paths home.

Dillis was looking out for them from the porch, the welcoming orb of the lit lamp behind her. She must have come to check that the trip to the mill had been a success.

'When it started getting dark—'

Emma was about to explain but James interrupted, glaring furiously. 'I'm not a child. Can't I go for a walk without having to give an account of myself? I won't be told where I may or may not go! That man,' he spat, 'he was the one who put the trap in our hedge!' And with that, he slammed his way into the house.

Dillis stared at Emma. 'What on earth has happened?'

Emma turned cold at the mention of the trap. Of course, that was why the man was familiar. But that had been a long time ago. Why speak of it now? Her chest still heaving from their walk, she gasped, 'We took a wrong turn coming back from the mill. I don't know how... Up on the hill, there was a man with a gun in the woods...'

A strange look passed over Dillis's face as she helped Emma off with her coat. 'On the hill? Have you never been warned? I suppose you'd not much cause to pass there when you came in the summer. Those woods are part of the Holwell Estate. You must have met the head gamekeeper, Malcolm Greep.'

'Gamekeeper?' Emma spluttered. 'We weren't poaching! We were lost and that was obvious. He was so unreasonable, Dillis. He threatened to shoot James!'

'Miss Emma.' Dillis's voice became urgent. 'Malcolm Greep doesn't care who you are or what you were doing on the Holwell Estate. You must promise me you will keep out of his way. If he takes against Master James, it will not go well. Malcolm Greep is a nasty piece of work and many a family round here can testify to his cruelty. He has his feet under the table with all those in power. Promise me, Miss Emma.'

'I-I-I promise.'

'What did Master James mean by a trap?'

'It was years ago, Dillis, I don't know why he brought it up.'

It had been a jolt to hear James refer to the incident. Emma had been surprised when he hadn't spoken of it at the time. But clearly he hadn't forgotten.

'Tell me, Miss Emma.'

'There was a trap. Out in the hedge, close to the house. A dead stoat was caught, and that man, Malcolm Greep, was there, collecting the poor creature. It was awful, and it really upset James. You know, just now,' Emma shook her head in bewilderment, 'he said we were living in *his* house. What did he mean?'

Dillis frowned as she remembered. 'He'd managed to get Lord Holwell interested in buying this place as a gamekeeper's lodge.' She sniffed. 'Far too good a house even for a head gamekeeper, but he was round here that autumn, all high and mighty, talking as if he owned it long before any agreements had been made.'

Emma was shocked. 'But Kersbrook is *our* house!'

Dillis nodded. 'That's the sort of man he is. Thinks the world owes him. He raged when he didn't get his way, but he's persistent. Lord Holwell approached your father several times about it. I heard it from one of the staff at the big house. And when Mr Linden passed, rest his soul, they were all sure your uncle would sell.' Dillis looked Emma right in the eye. 'Don't forget your promise, you and Master James must stay away from him.'

As Emma undressed for bed that night, she couldn't stop thinking about their encounter with the gamekeeper. She kneeled on the floor, pulling a cardboard box out from under her bed. James's old letters had arrived, packed with her books and the desk, and now she found herself wanting to read them. She climbed into bed, pulling the covers over her knees, and took out the uppermost letter.

'*If he takes against Master James...*' Dillis had warned.

It seemed Malcolm Greep already had.

**18**

*Devon, Summer Term 2023*

It's strange how some things take a while to click in your brain. It was seeing Rosie's face as she sat in the sunny garden that day that it struck me. Shooting hoops with Eddie had left me feeling better than I had in days. I hated to admit it, but I was missing playing sport. And I especially missed playing sport in all weathers.

That evening, I asked Mum about it. 'Can exercise and being outside help if you have mental health issues? I know it makes me feel good, but…'

Mum looked up from her book.

'Yeah, definitely. There's loads of research showing how exercise improves your mood. As well as being in green space, close to nature.'

I turned this over in my mind as I walked to school the following day. I was so busy thinking about it, that I didn't see Mr Harris on the stairwell until it was too late.

'Jude Simmons!' he bellowed. 'A word, please.'

I winced. 'Yes, Mr Harris.'

'Look here, Jude. Enough of this sulking about the academy. I won't have a fine young sportsman like you throwing away his talent. I've put your name down for the triathlon team. Your friend Amin does it. It's good fun. Not as serious as the Raptors, but there are plenty of competitions to enter if you want to. Thursdays, Jude, after school. I think it would suit you. Just give it a try, that's all I'm asking.'

How did he always manage to sound like he was telling you off, even when he was helping?

'I'll think about it,' I said.

'Good man.' He slapped me on the shoulder and strode off.

As I turned to go, I nearly bumped into Imogen. I gaped like a fish.

Photo.

Framed.

Kitchen.

My face was on fire.

But she didn't seem to notice. 'Hi, Jude. I was at Rosie's last night and she said you'd been over. It's really kind of you. You've cheered her up.'

I couldn't reply. I hadn't started visiting Rosie because I was kind; I'd wanted to make myself feel better about the academy. If anything, Rosie was the one who had been kind. She was seriously ill that first time I called round – she could have told me where to go, but she didn't. She'd listened and hadn't offered loads of opinions about me staking so much on the academy dream. I still felt a bit wobbly about it. Imogen stood waiting for me to say something, but how could I explain all that?

'See you later, then,' she said with a shrug, and disappeared in a crowd of kids.

Rosie was on the back step in her garden again that afternoon after school, rolling her gran's ammonite fossil between her fingers.

I told her about my meeting with Mr Harris.

'You should do it, Jude,' she said.

'I don't know...'

'What's the problem?'

'I've sort of lost my confidence. Does that make sense? You know, after being dropped from the team...'

'Totally makes sense, but this'll be different to the Raptors. Triathlon practice won't be any pressure. Maybe you need to remind yourself why you liked sport so much in the first place.'

'Maybe.' I looked out over the garden. Being with Rosie was so easy. I guess we'd become friends. 'Hey, I was wondering if you'd like to go for a walk along the coast path? We could go onto the cliffs, if you felt up to it? Check out some of that geology Mary Anning's so famous for?'

I've never seen anyone's face go white as quickly as Rosie's did then. She looked like someone had dropped a kettlebell on her foot.

'L-l-leave the house? No, I-I don't think I should, Jude.' If she'd been wearing her hoody, she would have pulled it over her head.

But I couldn't stop myself.

'Only, being outside and getting exercise is

142

supposed to be good for your mental health, Mum told me. And I'd be there.'

She looked at the floor. 'My key worker on the crisis team did say getting out might help.'

'You see. It's a good idea.'

She pulled the cuffs of her jumper over her fingertips. 'I don't know, Jude. What if I see someone from school?'

I thought of Mr Harris that morning, and his stern but kind words.

'You know what, Rosie Linden, I'll do you a deal. You come for a walk with me along the coast path and I'll go to triathlon tomorrow.'

I stuck out my hand to shake on it.

Rosie squeezed her eyes shut. I wasn't sure if she was about to cry.

But she took a deep breath, smiled and shook my hand.

'Deal.'

'All right then.' I smiled back.

Maddy took a bit of persuading, but seeing as Rosie's key worker had suggested it, she couldn't exactly argue.

Rosie wound the bright orange scarf around her

neck before we left. I must have raised an eyebrow as it wasn't scarf weather, because she said, 'Nice and bright, easy to find me if I get lost.'

We took a narrow cut-through between the houses which brought us out behind a row of beach huts. The sea was still. Gulls stood in the shallow water. I could see a group of kayakers further out. It was a sunny afternoon so there were lots of people, jogging, riding their bikes or walking their dogs.

'You okay?' I asked Rosie.

'Yeah, actually.' She smiled.

'Want to go on?'

She nodded. We took the steep cliff path, the edges thick with greenery. Rosie ran her hand through the waving seed heads as we wandered higher and higher.

At the top, I had to shield my eyes; the sun glistened on the water all the way to the horizon. Rosie held out a sprig of white flowers she'd picked from the verge.

'I found some flowers like these pressed between the pages of a book about holly trees. It was in that box of stuff my gran left me,' she said thoughtfully.

'I looked it up. It's called yarrow. It's a symbol for healing.'

I took the sprig. 'Did you find out what the old key was for?'

'Not a clue. I did locate those coordinates in the front of that book though. Old Brompton Road, right in the middle of London. Maybe Emma lived there? I was thinking about going to the library to look at some archives online and see if I can find out anything else. They've got free access. I just haven't felt up to it yet.'

We found a quiet bench and sat down.

Rosie gnawed at her lip. 'There are these videos on YouTube. My counsellor suggested I watch them. Other teenagers talking about their experiences of psychosis.' Rosie told me some of their stories – kids, just like me in every other way. Even though I'd seen what had happened to Rosie, I found it hard to put myself in their shoes. I couldn't imagine what it would be like to lose my grip on reality.

'My key worker says it can help to hear someone else's journey – explore the "what-ifs" of getting better at a safe distance. I can always press pause if it's too much.'

I wondered about those what-ifs. I was so sure Rosie was getting better. But what if I was wrong? What if she didn't get well again? What if she had another breakdown? And all the time, in the back of my mind, I wondered about that family history, and the way Rosie's gran had been when Rosie was on the bannister. What had she known about mental illness in the Linden family?

Rosie's gaze drifted out along the cliffs.

'It's amazing, all these layers of history in the rock. Reminds me of a book, like the layers are the pages, telling a story.' She turned to me. 'I keep thinking about Mary Anning. Where did she get her strength from to keep fighting them all? She must have really believed in herself. The ideas I had when I went missing *still* feel so real. How can I trust myself again?'

I racked my brains for something to say. In the end, I picked up her hand and placed the yarrow in her palm. Yarrow for healing.

As we walked along her road on the return leg, Rosie said, 'Thanks for making me come out, Jude. You were totally right, it felt really good.'

I laughed, rolling my eyes. 'I'd better get ready for triathlon, then.'

At her house, Maddy did a great job of pretending she hadn't been watching for us coming back the entire time.

**19**

*Kersbrook, Easter 1888*

Olivier arrived the week before Easter, heading up a convoy of carts filled to bursting with the new sprouting greenery of saplings. He looked like a rajah leading a procession of elephants. The trees had come all the way from the famous Lucombe Nurseries in Exeter, each one ordered according to James's list. It took them most of the morning to unload them. Mr Kerr sniffed and stomped off to his fields, but Dillis thought it was a marvellous scheme.

'Olivier, it's wonderful to have you back with us,' Emma cried as he swung down from the cart. She was glad to see him – there were things they needed to discuss about James's condition, but that could wait. 'How's Oxford? How did you do in your exams?'

'Fine, fine.' He brushed away her questions. 'It's good to see you both. Your letters are charming, Emma, but it's not the same as being here.'

She smiled as Olivier put his arms across their shoulders, and the three of them walked towards the house. 'We have some news, don't we, James?'

'Indeed. You remember the old rowing boat we used to swim from, and how we couldn't find what happened to it last summer?'

'Of course!'

'James discovered it under a heap of overgrown brambles by one of the outbuildings. It mustn't have been put away properly and had been out in all weathers. It was in a very sorry state.' Emma cast a conspiratorial look in James's direction.

'We've been working hard, haven't we, Em—'

'I won't take any credit,' she interrupted, laughing. 'It has all been James.' She smiled up at Olivier. 'All of it!'

James *had* worked hard on the boat, patiently sanding it and repairing the holes in the hull. It had given him a purpose through the dark winter months, and Emma watched as each day her brother seemed to come back to his old self, just as he brought about the same change in the boat. They rarely ventured far from the house, except to collect flour from the mill. Now they were familiar with the path, Emma was glad there was little likelihood of meeting Malcolm Greep again.

'That is not true, Emma,' James insisted. 'Your painting skills were just as important.'

'Oh, but that was only the finishing touch!'

'Don't listen to a word of it, Olivier.'

Olivier looked between them as they talked back and forth, clearly relieved to have returned to such merriment.

'Finishing touch?' he asked, grinning. 'So, is it complete?'

'Yes! And you have arrived in perfect time for the launch,' declared James. 'The fishermen forecast fine weather for tomorrow and Mr Kerr has agreed to lend us his donkey and cart.'

'James has baked an apple cake in honour of the occasion and we shall have a picnic.'

'Baked an apple cake? James, I hardly know you. This is going to be quite the Easter holidays I can tell!' laughed Olivier.

That afternoon, James lifted a patch of turf in the garden and dug a deep hole. Olivier lowered in a beech sapling and James filled the hole with soil, tamping it down with his boots so it would grow straight.

'The first of many,' he announced. He was determined to spend the rest of the day planting more and more trees. Finding his friend happily occupied, Olivier went to study indoors.

Emma stood in the doorway, watching James's progress.

'He looks well, but he is still ill, Olivier.'

Olivier raised his head from the notes he was making.

'He tries hard to hide it, but I can see him concentrating. It's as if someone is speaking to him and he's listening, and he begins to reply and then catches himself. The room is empty and quiet, but for him, it's full of sounds, voices perhaps, and things I cannot see. It's as if we are in different worlds while together in the same space.'

Olivier put down his pen. 'Do you ever ask him what he sees or hears?'

Emma shook her head with a sad smile. 'He won't admit he hears or sees anything. I don't think it's painful or disturbing, but he's embarrassed when he sees me looking.'

'These delusions and hallucinations may always be present to some extent, Emma.'

She nodded, slowly. He'd answered the question that had been bothering her, but he was only confirming what she'd already guessed.

'Does he find the sedatives help?' Olivier asked.

Emma shook her head again. 'He doesn't take them. He says he can't think. They make him weak as a kitten.'

She found herself wondering if her mother had resisted medicine in the same way.

The promise was etched in the desk, *I will keep you safe.* If James could know something of Mother's illness, it *might* help. Emma thought again of the locked drawer in the study. She had put it out of her mind, the shadow of her father's disapproval looming large. And most likely, there was nothing there... But if so, why lock the drawer?

It occurred to her that she had never asked Dillis about her mother. Would she know anything? It

152

would be simpler than breaking into the desk. Yes, speaking to Dillis would be better. Emma resolved to ask at the next opportunity.

The sunset that evening was a dazzling of pinks and golds behind the hills and still James kept planting, ignoring Emma's pleas to stop for the night. At last, when it was too dark to see the end of his spade, he came inside, flopping onto the floor at Emma's feet in the conservatory, announcing that he needed to straighten out his back after digging. Olivier laughed at him from where he sat on the couch, surrounded by books.

'You'll have all the trees planted by the time I'm here in the summer holidays if you continue at this pace!'

'That's my plan.' James sat up, grinning.

It was so good to see them chatting like this, the way they always used to. And even better, Olivier was planning to spend the summer with them. It would be like old times.

True to the fishermen's forecast, the next day dawned fine and dry. James and Olivier lifted the boat onto the cart, keel skyward, the picnic tucked underneath. Dillis walked with Emma behind, a basket of eggs hanging from her arm. She would come with them as far as the beach road and then go on with her deliveries. Emma felt light and free, strolling between the hedgerows to the rhythm of the donkey's clinking bridle.

'You are a different child,' said Dillis. 'More a young lady really.'

'I know. It's Kersbrook,' replied Emma. 'It heals us all.' She paused. The boys were a little way ahead. It was now or never… 'Dillis, what do you remember of my mother?'

Dillis pulled up short. 'I wondered when you might ask.'

'I want to hear everything.'

She nodded, slowly. 'Well, it isn't much. You know your mother was born in Calcutta?'

Emma's eyes widened. 'No, but James did say something about a captain in the East India Company.'

'That would be your grandfather, John Hayes. I

was only a girl when he married your grandmother, Lizzie, and they moved to India with the Company. He passed away out there so I never saw him again. I heard my father once say he had an old soul. I like that expression, means he was sensitive and wise beyond his years. In my mind, he is the picture of Master James.'

Emma watched James strolling ahead of them, as Dillis went on. 'Kersbrook's always been in the Hayes family, as far as I know, so your grandmother returned here. Your mother, well, she must have been twelve or thirteen then. I was too busy to pay much attention. Harold and I were to be married, and taking on the farm from his parents.' She frowned. 'A pretty, light-haired girl is what I remember of Marianne.'

'Marianne?' Emma's hand leaped to her mouth. Her mother's name had been Marianne!

'Heaven help us,' groaned Dillis. 'Your father even kept that from you, did he?'

'What else?' Emma *had* to know more.

But Dillis shook her head sadly. 'That's about it, my lover. Your grandmother died not long after your mother, broken hearted, by my reckoning.

That was when your father started bringing you children down for the summer. But the things I'm sure you really want to know – what happened to her, her illness,' Dillis looked straight at Emma, 'that, I don't know.'

Emma sighed. To know the name of her mother, the person who had inscribed that promise, *I will keep you safe*, was precious beyond measure. But James needed details to guide him through his illness and Dillis had none. Emma decided not to stir up more sadness by telling him the fragments she'd learned.

Deep in thought, Emma would never have paid any attention to the cottage at the crossroads, but a sudden movement at the window caught her eye. The building was like the Kerrs' farmhouse, white walls topped with thick thatch. Yellow primroses speckled the garden. A slight girl around Emma's age looked out and then she was gone, turning away into the room as if startled by being spotted.

'Who lives there? I'm sure I saw a young girl.'

'Oh, that's Major Willard and his daughter Annie.' Dillis lowered her voice. 'Right sad tale that is and I don't mind saying. She's his only daughter.

His wife died after the birth, I believe. He took the cottage only six months ago for his retirement, intending to while away his days strolling by the sea, but it wasn't to be. The Major suffered apoplexy of the brain the night he arrived. Doctor Gregory was called but there was nothing to be done. He's confined to his bed and that poor girl is confined to the house as his nurse.' Dillis sniffed and shifted the basket of eggs to her other arm.

'She must be lonely.'

'So would you be in her place.' Dillis shook her head, then pointed to a path leading inland. 'Righto, this is me. Behave yourselves and bring home some fish for your tea. One thing I don't have to teach you is how to fillet and cook them – you've spent enough summers messing about on the beach.' She gave a brisk wave as she left on her errands.

Emma ran to catch up with the boys. 'Olivier, what is apoplexy of the brain?'

'A bleed. It can cause paralysis and loss of speech. Why do you ask?'

'Oh, no reason. Just something I heard.'

They arrived at the top of the hill looking over the beach. Sky merged with sea in a warm, wavering haze. Fishing boats had been pulled up high for the spring tide. They made their way carefully down the track. Sunlight dazzled from every surface. The salty sea breeze tingled Emma's cheeks.

She tethered the donkey to a stake on a patch of grass while James and Olivier rolled up their trousers. They lifted the boat out to where the water was deep enough to take her. She bobbed merrily on the waves.

'She floats!' called James jubilantly. 'Come on, let's try her out.'

He waded back for Emma, giving her a piggy-back to the boat. Once she was settled, he hopped in beside her, rowing in circles. Olivier swam beside them.

'What do you think, Em?' James demanded.

She laughed. 'Good as new!'

'Ha! Better than new.'

'All right, take me to shore now. I want to hunt for fossils.'

'I didn't think there were any on this part of the coast? Don't you have to go further up, to the Blue Lias rocks where your Mary Anning lived?' he quizzed her.

'Actually, there are. Mostly fossilised shells. I want to find the ones shaped like butterfly wings. Now put me to shore, please.'

The butterfly-like brachiopods weren't exactly *ichthyosaur* remains, but Emma found them just as exciting. Who knew what lay hidden in the rocks? Perhaps a previously unknown dinosaur was waiting to be uncovered and shared with the world for the benefit of science, just like Mary had done. And then there were the pebbles. She couldn't help wonder about the difference between the red cliffs and the pebble beach. The pebbles were nothing like the cliff rock, so where had they come from?

The water was icy cold on her feet as she jumped down and waded through the shallows to the beach. She stood for a while watching James and Olivier messing about in the boat, getting their fishing lines tangled and roaring with laughter. Her heart soared to see them together. Suddenly Annie Willard's pale face rose in her mind. Was she lonely? All that time confined in her attic kingdom in London, Emma had never really felt alone. She'd had her books, her letters from James and always the prospect of their summers in Devon. Perhaps, as they were going to be staying in Kersbrook, if she could find a way to meet Annie, they might be friends.

At lunchtime, the boys rowed ashore, and they spread their picnic at the high tide mark. James's apple cake was a triumph. Arriving at the house later that afternoon, Dillis approved of the mackerel James presented for inspection. She was less impressed with the smooth pebbles filling Emma's pockets. Dillis didn't hold with keeping anything that wasn't useful or edible.

'They're made from hard quartzite,' Emma explained at her quizzical expression. 'Did you know the pebbles here are identical to those found in Brittany? I have a theory they come from the same source. I love their colours, and their shapes, smoothed by the waves. I'm going to draw them in my sketchbook.'

'Imagine if everyone shifted the pebbles away like that,' Dillis scolded. 'There'd be none left on the beach!' But Emma noticed with a smile that Dillis took a small pale blue one and put it in her pocket.

*Devon, Summer Term 2023*

The first shock of the afternoon was walking up the
slope to triathlon practice behind Imogen.

'Oh, hi, Jude,' she said, waiting for me to catch
up. 'You joining the team?'

'Uh, hi, Imogen. Yeah, Mr Harris said to come
along.' Who knew she even *did* triathlon?

The second shock was seeing Zak Riley and his
minions hanging out on the railings leading to the
Astroturf. I could *not* believe it. I don't know the
minions' names, but they have the same haircut and
the same sneery look on their faces. It's like trying
to tell identical triplets apart. That's why Amin calls
them the minions – interchangeable underlings for a
despicable villain. If you hadn't guessed, the villain
is Zak.

The Astroturf is not Zak's natural habitat, nothing to do with physical activity is. So I knew that he'd somehow found out I'd signed up for triathlon, and he was here to make a massive deal out of it.

I was hoping they wouldn't notice us as we went past. Making awkward conversation with Imogen *and* getting back to sport were stressful enough, the last thing I needed was Zak Riley's thoughts on the subject. But he was in the mood for sharing, and loudly.

'How's the girlfriend, Simple Simmons?' Zak called out as we got close. 'How's Loopy Linden?' he sneered.

Imogen shot me a look.

I shook my head vigorously. 'We're not, honest.'

'Not what, Simple Simmons? Not in lurve?' The minions laughed.

'Bet Loopy Linden's grateful for anyone taking an interest now she's off her rocker. Even Simple Simmons, academy reject,' Zak scoffed.

Imogen's eyes narrowed. 'What have you been saying about Rosie?' she hissed.

'Nothing!' But she stormed off towards practice.

The minions were making smooching sounds and thought they were hilarious. I could tell I was turning bright, screaming red, which they found even more funny.

Luckily, Amin showed up at that precise moment. I don't know what it is about Amin, but his very existence seems to wipe the smirk off Zak's face. They live round the corner from each other, and I'm sure there's history, but Amin won't tell me.

'Everything all right here?' Amin asked, scanning our faces.

'Just welcoming the latest recruit to the team,' said Zak, sliding off the railing. 'But we're going now.' He picked up his bag. 'Have a good time, Jude.'

He blew me a kiss and they slunk off.

Amin slung his arm over my shoulders, steering me towards where everyone was warming up. 'Mate, you let him get to you and it's game over. You have *got* to ignore him.'

'B-b-but, he's so infuriating!' I exploded. 'You should have heard what he was saying about Rosie.'

Amin stopped and, as he often did, spelled things out for me. 'Mate, there are things you do not want to know about Zak's life. His dad is a specimen. Zak's evolved like that just to survive his homelife. Ig. Nore. Him,' he finished as we joined the rest of the team.

Imogen glared at me. 'For the record, Jude, if you hurt Rosie in *any* way, I will personally oversee your execution.'

Hurt Rosie? I stared back at her helplessly. 'But we're not even...'

Amin's eyebrows shot skywards. I shook my head at him, I'd fill him in later.

I pulled on my trainers. How'd I manage to make such a mess of things? Flippin' Zak. Fortunately, racing around the Astroturf and being yelled at by Mr Harris were *exactly* what I needed to get my head straight.

'So, how did it go?' Rosie asked, the day after the training session.

'Yeah, good. Loads of fun. And it turns out that Imogen does triathlon too.'

'Didn't you know that?'

'Nope. I haven't talked to Imogen for ages, but we talked yesterday. Kind of. It was great being with Amin.'

'Why haven't you talked to Imogen? Aren't your mums friends?' Rosie looked intrigued.

I nodded and scrunched up my face. It was so embarrassing. But I knew Rosie would understand. 'There's this stupid photo...'

And I told her. Of course, she found it funny.

'Seriously? We've all got photos like that from being babies, Jude. Mum's got pictures of me completely starkers on the beach with my cousins. Parents are clueless like that.'

'Really?' I was genuinely surprised.

'Yes!' she snorted. 'So will you go back?'

'To triathlon?'

'Yeah.'

'I think I will. Anyway,' I said, changing the subject, 'what's this?' I pointed to a notebook beside her, covered with writing and sketches of what looked like shells.

She blushed. 'I've been geeking out on fossils.'

I raised an eyebrow. 'You've been bitten by the Mary Anning bug, then? Can I see?'

165

Once I'd promised faithfully not to laugh at her drawing skills, which wasn't a problem as they were great, she showed me what she'd been researching.

'I didn't think there were any exciting fossils down our end of the coast, but look at these.' She pointed to her pictures, radiating lines imprinted on rock-like wings. 'They're a type of extinct brachiopod, ancient shellfish. They're so beautiful. Guess what their local name is?'

I shrugged.

Rosie laughed. 'Butterflies!'

21

I'd been kind of bullied into taking a place at the East Devon Summer Triathlon a few weeks later. Amin and Imogen were doing it and had persuaded me to compete. It involved a sea swim, a cycle around town and a flat, fast sprint along the prom. It was a good one for beginners. The sun shone and there were big blue skies. I was already enjoying myself – it felt good to be doing something competitive. I kicked out my legs and shook my arms, trying to keep my muscles warm and moving like Mr Harris had told us. People milled around, flags fluttering in the breeze, and the race's sponsor was handing out free soft drinks – there was a buzz in the air.

Everyone was excited. Mum had come to watch and she'd brought Rosie too. That walk up to the clifftop had been a turning point – we'd been out on loads of walks since, along the beach below the cliffs, tapping rocks for 'butterflies', but she was nervous of being on her own. She and Mum were going to wait at the finish line to see us over. Rosie looked a bit overwhelmed and I hoped she would be all right, but I knew Mum would take care of her. She seemed so much better.

Suddenly, through the crowd, I spotted somebody in a pair of green overalls.

'That's Alice! Look!' I grabbed hold of Rosie.

Sure enough, there was Alice, standing under a gazebo by an ambulance, appearing just as capable and just as kind as she had that day on the high street.

'Jude! Are you racing?' She was delighted to see us.

'Yeah, number forty-five. Are you working?'

'Yeah, I'm part of the first aid team. In case of emergencies.' I must have looked uneasy then because she added, 'There normally aren't any, don't worry. A sprained ankle or a bit of heat exhaustion. It's usually fine.'

Rosie was staring blankly between us and I realised that she didn't remember Alice. 'Oh, I'm sorry, Rosie. This is Alice, she's the paramedic who helped you when you got ill. She was amazing, Rosie, honest.'

'Oh, um, hi. I mean, thanks. I...' Rosie looked awkwardly at her feet.

'No thanks needed,' said Alice brightly. 'It's my job. And if any were needed, it's thanks enough to see you so well.' She reached out and gently squeezed Rosie's arm. 'Besides, it's this guy who did the heavy lifting.'

'I know,' she said quietly.

I rolled my eyes. Rosie had described me as her anchor that day, but I knew what an anchor she had been to me since. Sometimes I wondered how I would have come out of that time of disappointment and failure without her.

'Jude! Come on!' Mr Harris bellowed, beckoning me to join the rest of the team.

I grinned at Rosie. 'See you at the finish line.'

She nodded. 'Enjoy it, Jude. Remember to enjoy it.'

I gave her a thumbs up and ran off.

Me and Amin stood next to each other at the start of the race. I was getting a bit jittery, reminding me how I used to be in the minutes before a match.

I just wanted to get going. Then Amin caught my eye, his face serious. 'Mate, I wanted to tell you I was wrong about Rosie. You were right. Seeing her today, she's... normal.'

What a moment to have a heart-to-heart, jostling among the other competitors.

I shook my head. 'Nah, Rosie's not normal. She's *ab*normally kind and brave, though I get what you mean.'

He nodded, surprised, but in a good way, and then the starter gun went off, and all hell broke loose.

I'm blaming Amin for distracting me, because I began badly on the swimming section. I've never been in such a tangle of bodies, legs and arms flailing. Mr Harris had warned me what it would be like, but nothing prepared me for the real thing. His technique training went out the window. My only option was to act like some kind of marine combine harvester. At one point I thought I might drown. And even once my stroke got going, there was no way of catching Amin and his massive paddle hands. I messed up my transfer onto the bike. It was like I didn't know what the pedals were for.

170

But running was where I did best. I've always been speedy, and I made up time, overtaking the people who'd had their elbows in my ribs during the swim.

Mum came in for a flying hug at the finishing line and Rosie beamed at me. I came twentieth, which I was pleased with considering it was my first race. But the main thing was, it had been fun.

Mr Harris was elated with his team.

'Pizza at the Waterfront for anyone who can stay! On me!' he declared.

The Waterfront is a restaurant on the old docks and it wasn't far from the finishing line of the race. Mum, me, Rosie, Amin and Imogen all went. The weather was still perfect, so we grabbed a table outside, the water glinting in the late afternoon sun. Sandwiched together on one side of the bench, me, Imogen and Amin laughed and marvelled by turn at how we had done in the race. Now that we'd got our breath back, we were buoyant with success, full of stories of the other competitors' dodgy tactics and poor technique, stories that got wilder the more we talked. Rosie sat opposite, listening and laughing from time to time, but saying very little.

Once we'd quietened down and were filling up on pizza, I noticed Mr Harris sitting next to Mum. They seemed to be getting on very well, laughing and chatting. I decided not to think about that too much – life was just getting back to normal.

Rosie didn't seem hungry and Amin finished her pizza.

'What?!' he'd exclaimed. 'Can't let good pizza go to waste!'

I winked at her. She smiled but she seemed preoccupied.

Later, once he'd paid the bill, Mr Harris got me on my own for a discreet chat.

'Jude, the county coach had his eye on you in that race. He was impressed. I know you made a few mistakes, but he asked me to sound you out about trying for the county.'

I opened my mouth, but he raised a hand to silence me.

'I know you've only recently joined the school team and I don't want you to feel rushed into anything. But, you see, all that training with the Raptors wasn't wasted. You're good, Jude, really good. What do you think about taking triathlon more seriously?'

I looked over at Rosie and found her watching us. She raised her eyebrows questioningly. If I hadn't already known my own mind, that sealed it for me.

'I'm not saying never, Mr Harris, but I'm just starting to enjoy sport again. I want to do it for fun for a bit longer. Do you mind?'

Mr Harris shook his head. 'Not at all.' He put his hand on my shoulder. 'It seems that you're starting to get to know yourself. I'm glad you're making your own choices. Let's see how things pan out, shall we?'

'So, meet at mine tomorrow? Ten sound okay?' asked Imogen.

We could have sat there all night, laughing and dissecting the race, so when she offered to make us pancakes the next day, we jumped at it. Especially Amin – there's not much he won't do for a chocolate and banana pancake.

'Yup, perfect.' I nodded. I'd go to Rosie's beforehand and walk her over. But for now, I'd promised Maddy I'd get her home safely.

After telling Mum that I wouldn't be back late, me and Rosie walked to her house along the river.

'Your mum is cool. You get on well, don't you?'

'Yeah, she's brilliant,' I replied.

'Are you sore from the race?'

'Not too bad,' I lied. I'd been trying not to wince. My muscles felt like floppy spaghetti, but it was worth it.

We walked along, not talking, but not really needing to either.

'Hope you don't mind me saying,' I said after a while, 'but you've been quiet today. Didn't you enjoy the race?'

Rosie blinked. 'Oh no, it wasn't that. You were all brilliant.'

'So what is it?'

She stopped walking and rummaged around in her backpack, handing me a long crisp envelope. 'This. Read it.'

It was an official looking letter, headed with the address and logo of a local solicitor's firm.

### The Last Will and Testament of Grace Linden.

'It's my Gran's will,' she said in a small voice. 'Take a look.'

'Okay…'

```
   I, Grace Linden, being of sound
mind, and not acting under duress,
fraud or undue influence of any
person, hereby make, publish and
declare this my last Will and
Testament, and expressly hereby
revoke any and all other Wills and
Codicils heretofore made by me.
```

I skipped through Article One. Something about Executors.

'This bit.' Rosie pointed to the section at the bottom of the page.

**Article Two**

```
I give and bequeath to my daughter
Madeline, my house (10 Albion
Street), all of my clothing, personal
effects, furniture and household
furnishings, car and other tangible
personal property owned by me at the
time of my decease.
```

```
    I give and bequeath to my grand-
daughter Rosie, Kersbrook House, its
entire contents, and its attached
stipendiary.
```

I had to read it twice.

'Your gran left you a house?'

From under her T-shirt, Rosie pulled on a cord around her neck and held up a brass object. The key from the envelope in her gran's box.

'This is the front door key.'

**22**

Rosie untied the cord, letting it drop into my hand. A front door key!

'Mum's furious Gran had a secret like this and didn't tell anyone,' she said.

'I bet.'

'We never had reason to suspect. The house isn't far away so she could have easily spent time there while we were at school and work. Mum said Gran was always very social when they were growing up, so it never occurred to her that she might not have been helping with coffee mornings or doing flower arranging as she said she was. Though Grandad must have known.' Rosie shook her head. 'Apparently it's secluded, out in the countryside, further up the coast, so the chances of anyone coming across her there were pretty low.' She sighed. 'Mum says it's like Gran was living a double life.'

'What do you think?' I asked.

'I don't know. I mean, why'd Gran keep it secret in the first place? I'm sad she didn't feel she could tell us about it.'

I shook my head. 'Seriously, Rosie... a house? You're thirteen. How are you going to cover the bills?'

'That's all paid for by this stipendiary-thing in the will.' She shrugged. I could see she thought it was unbelievable too. 'It's a pot of money that the solicitors keep. It pays for everything, even repairs, like if there's a leak in the roof.'

She looked at me. 'Jude, I want to go. But not with Mum when she's being so cross about it. Do you remember those woods they were gonna level for a new road at Holwell Hill? It's near there, close to the cafe at the old mill at Little Down.'

I vaguely knew where she meant.

'I was wondering if you'd come with me? We could cycle there.'

I couldn't answer fast enough. 'I'd love to, Rosie. I wonder what it's like. Maybe it's a mansion? A castle?'

She laughed. 'I don't think so from what the solicitor says. Some people called Naomi and Dan

Kerr live at the farm next door and have helped keep an eye on it. Apparently it's been in Gran's family for generations. I'm hoping it might give me some answers.'

I smiled back uneasily. The secrets in Rosie's family history were just getting bigger.

There was paperwork with the solicitor to sort out so we couldn't go until the following weekend.

In the meantime, Amin and Imogen were as shocked as I was.

'A whole house?' Amin asked, shooting a hoop in Rosie's back garden.

Maddy had taken Eddie to his swimming lesson and Rob was at work, so Rosie didn't mind talking about it. And I *needed* to talk about it. 'Who has a house at our age? It's incredible.'

Imogen, sitting next to Rosie in the sun on the back step, hooked her arm through Rosie's. 'I think it's lovely. It's as though your gran's looking out for you, providing for you after she's gone – like a guardian angel.'

'Lovely and *useful*,' grinned Amin. 'Might be the perfect venue for a film night!' He had a catalogue of niche indie films he was determined to inflict on us.

We set off on our bikes early that Saturday. Rosie and I knew our printed-out map by heart. There would be no mistaking the house, the only building after the farm, standing on its own.

Once you pass the Recycling Centre on the edge of town, Kersbrook is a couple of miles along narrow country lanes. On your right, you catch glimpses of the sea whenever there's a field gate. You turn off at an old stone cross covered in ivy, and there's the lane down to Kersbrook – narrow and lined by tall hedgerows like thick green walls, a leafy tunnel to a lost land. You can't see the sea from there, but you can smell its saltiness. As we free-wheeled down into the valley, patchy sunlight flickering over my handlebars, I found myself glancing over my shoulder, half expecting the way to have closed behind us. Everything about that cycle ride made the hairs on the back of my neck stand up and the feeling was stronger the closer we got.

On the left, we passed the whitewashed walls and thatched roof of Kersbrook Farm – the name etched on a sign beside the door. A shallow stream gushed over the road and we cycled slowly across the ford, spray sloshing up from our tyres. Then, at last, we saw the house. Only its lower storey windows and triangular-roofed porch were visible through the thick band of trees. Though we knew this had to be it, we still checked the print-out to be sure.

We leaned our bikes against a wall made from pebbles, like giant bubble wrap. Lots of walls round our way are made like that. Rosie had been reading an original paper from the Victorian times, and told me how the pebblebed was deposited here from Brittany by an ancient river in the Triassic Period.

On the other side, the ground was higher, so where we stood, the bases of the trees around the house were at head height, making me feel like Jack surveying the fairy-tale beanstalk. We opened the green wooden gate onto some steps. Birds sang everywhere. Sunlight filtered through the trees in beams. It was like an enchanted house in the woods.

The grass had been left to grow long and the garden was full of flowers and the sound of humming insects. A gravel path led to the porch door.

We didn't say anything. It all felt unreal. Kersbrook seemed to have sunk into the ground with its low roof. It looked homely and kind of comfy. Rosie and I raised our eyebrows at each other. We were both holding our breath.

The porch door wasn't locked. On the windowsills were pots of red flowers, pretty sure they were geraniums – Mum would've known. There was a narrow wooden bench and a metal bootjack for taking off your shoes. Rosie took out her key. Her hands were shaking.

'I feel like I'll open the door and there'll be people inside,' she whispered.

I knew what she meant. I could almost hear laughter. It was spooky, but I wasn't afraid.

'Want me to do it?'

She shook her head and turned the key. The door swung open. The smell of old wood and polish hit us straight away.

Rosie paused beside a table in the hall. There was a framed black and white photo of a woman with light curly hair, smiling at a man who looked directly at the camera. She picked it up. 'My gran when she was young. Jude, this is Grace.' She turned to me with a smile.

'And who's that with her?' The way Grace looked at him was like she was seeing him for the last time – loving and sad, all mixed together.

'I don't know.'

Rosie slowly replaced the photograph and followed the corridor through the house. The wooden floor creaked with each step. Over the walls clustered framed drawings of plants, shells and fossils. On a peg in the kitchen hung an old-fashioned apron, as if someone from long ago had just popped out for a pint of milk. In the conservatory, a desk and a chair stood on a faded patterned rug, looking over the garden. Apart from a paved terrace outside and the lawn beyond, there were trees everywhere, reaching up to the blue sky.

'Hello.' A voice called to us through the house, making us both jump.

A woman with a baby in a sling on her front walked into the room. 'Hello!'

'Hello, I'm Rosie Linden...'

'Rosie! It's lovely to meet you at last. I'm Naomi Kerr from the farm. Your gran told me and Dan so much about you. How do you like Kersbrook?'

Naomi wasn't what I was expecting. She wore bright red dungarees and had dimples when she smiled. I'd imagined an old lady in a flowery dress and a pinny. She gave Rosie and me warm side hugs around the baby.

'I didn't know anything about the house,' Rosie said quietly.

Naomi nodded. 'No, you wouldn't have done. This is the way it's always been, a secret retreat. It nearly got sold once, I think, a long time ago, by someone in the family who didn't understand how much history there is. As well as happiness, there's been sadness here—'

'What do you mean?' asked Rosie, her eyes wide.

Naomi shook her head. 'A young man and an awful accident, but I know nothing more than that. It was a long time ago. Your gran said the house must be kept secret so it would always be here for those who need it. And I think, maybe, you do?' She smiled and I saw straightaway that she understood. 'It's pretty much unaltered since Victorian times.

184

Your gran had electricity put in and there's a septic tank now, but other than that...'

Rosie sat down on an old couch with a wooden frame, the colours faded by the sun.

'I've got an apple cake over at the farmhouse. I can bring some milk and we could have a cup of tea. How about I do that and give you time to look around?' suggested Naomi gently.

I thought cake was an amazing idea. I was suddenly starving. Rosie smiled and nodded.

'Thanks.'

I sat down beside her. 'What do you think to that? Some awful accident...'

Rosie raised her eyebrows. 'Y'know what else is strange? These drawings of fossils and rocks, all the stuff on the windowsills. Makes me think how those books from Gran's box would fit in here, especially the one on Mary Anning.' She pursed her lips. 'I need to find out who Emma Linden was and more importantly... what she's got to do with me.'

That summer there was a heat wave. We broke up from school on the 24th of July and it already felt like it had been going on for weeks. Even with the windows open, the classrooms were as stuffy as anything.

'Yahoooo! Summer holidays!' shouted Amin, running out of double maths at the end of the day and kicking his school bag in the air.

There was a loud crack as it landed on the hard floor. I winced. From the puddle of water that began seeping out, he'd obviously smashed his water bottle. Amin didn't care. He ripped open the bag and tipped the remaining water over his head.

'Come on!' I yelled, laughing at the sight of him.

We were seeing Imogen and Rosie at the main gates and I didn't want to keep Rosie waiting. She hadn't been back to school yet, and this was the first time she'd come to meet us. She was looking around nervously as kids streamed out, celebrating the start of the holidays like we'd just survived the apocalypse.

Amin threw his arms around their shoulders. 'Summer's here!'

'Oh, you're wet,' said Imogen, shaking him off.

Rosie giggled.

'Imogen.' Amin grinned. 'How can you care about a bit of water when we have the whole summer holidays ahead of us? And we have some serious plans!'

Rosie smiled at me. The 'serious plans' were pretty straightforward. We were going to spend every day of the holidays at Kersbrook, exploring the countryside on our bikes and going down to the beach.

Something funny had happened between the four of us that summer term – we'd sort of become inseparable. It was partly to do with the triathlon team, Rosie being ill, me getting over that stupid photograph and a shared love of pancakes. It also helped that Rosie had somewhere we could hang out. Kersbrook had become a part of our lives. I still found it amazing that Rosie's gran had kept this gift a secret, as though she were keeping it especially for her. I wondered if Rosie had never been ill, whether it might have stayed secret, waiting for the next Linden who needed it most.

We'd worked hard to clear the grounds which had got overgrown while Rosie's gran had been ill. But that night, we were allowed to stay over, after much nagging of our parents. They finally caved in when Dan Kerr from the farm kindly offered to kip on the sofa in the conservatory. Little Daisy was up so much in the night teething, he reckoned he'd have a better chance at a full night's sleep with us. The conditions were, one night *only* and we had to sleep in separate rooms. It was a massive deal and we were super excited about it.

We cycled over to Kersbrook with bags of supplies on our backs. Cycling along the lanes with my friends, the sun low in the sky and the breeze in my hair, life felt good. And then there was Kersbrook. The house was just the way it always looked, warm and welcoming among the trees.

We left our bikes leaning against the wall at the front of the house. After the excitement of getting there, we paused by the gate. It felt like a big moment, the four of us together, the summer stretching ahead. Then we started grinning and Amin grabbed the key from Rosie and charged off to open up.

Later, Rosie and I were in the kitchen unpacking the food we'd brought. Being at Kersbrook, the feeling of history was everywhere, like it was happening just out of earshot.

'Did you find anything out about Emma Linden?'

'I did actually,' Rosie replied. 'She was my great-great-grandmother. One of the librarians was really helpful and I found a record of Emma living here at Kersbrook in 1891. But it seemed like the house had been in the family long before that and they might have even built it. They were the Hayes. Is this boring?'

'Absolutely not. Anything come up about an accident?'

'No, but there was something about Emma's grandfather, John Hayes, he disappeared mysteriously in India—'

We were interrupted by Amin tearing into the kitchen, Imogen hot on his heels. 'You are never going to believe what we've found in one of the sheds out there!'

His face was alight.

'A boat!' interrupted Imogen. 'There's a rowing boat.'

'What? Really?' Rosie stood up.

'Come and see,' called Imogen, already heading off.

'Let's fix it up and take it down to the beach.' Amin pounded my back.

The shed was one of the whitewashed outbuildings along the top end of the house. This part of the building hadn't been connected to electricity, but even in the evening shadows we could make out the shape of a rowing boat. The paint was peeling and it was propped up on wooden stands, keel pointing towards the ceiling. Somebody had been careful to put it away properly.

'What do you think, Rosie?' asked Amin eagerly. 'It looks all right, doesn't it? Shall we fix it up?'

Rosie stroked the woodwork then looked at him with shining eyes. 'Yeah, let's!'

**23**

*Kersbrook, Summer 1888*

The boat tilted alarmingly to one side as James's beaming face appeared over the rim, dripping with sea water.

'It's wonderful, Em. You should learn to swim.'

It was over a week since the launch and they had spent every day at the beach. Emma put her book down. 'That's all very well for you to say, it's not the same for girls. When boys break the rules, they're courageous, when girls do the same, they're odd.'

'Pfff!' he said dismissively. 'What are you reading anyway?' He flicked up the cover. '*The Natural History of Ilex Aquifoleum.* A history of the holly tree? How can you bear to read books like this, Emma? Father barricaded you in with science and now you read it of your own choosing. As if dry facts alone could describe the world!' His face was disdainful. 'Doesn't it make you angry? The way he treated us? We were a family of clockwork automatons, feelings not permitted. And much good it did any of us!'

His words surprised her. She had never heard him speak like this about their father. She snatched the book away, no ready answer to give him. She loved to understand the way the world worked. If anything, it made the world more beautiful. But she could see he was right, there was more to life than diagrams and facts. Possibly even fossils. She sighed and looked over the edge at the glistening water. It was tempting. Could she learn to swim? Emma felt suddenly bold. Whyever not!

'Hey, who's that?' He pointed to the hill overlooking the beach. A girl stood there, the breeze catching her white dress.

Emma sat up, shielding her eyes.

'I think it's the girl from the cottage at the crossroads, I saw her at the window. Do you remember, Dillis told me about her?'

'Come on, let's go and say hello. Olivier!' James called. 'We're going to say hello to...' He turned back to Emma. 'What's her name?'

'Annie.'

'... to Annie!'

Emma smiled at his fit of friendliness – so like his old self. She'd wondered about being friends with Annie. This might be her chance.

James swam round to the prow, taking hold of the mooring rope and pulling the boat the few short metres back to shore. When the keel ground on the pebbles, Emma lifted up her skirts, jumped out and waded the last bit to dry land. It really *would* be lovely to shed these silly clothes and be free like the boys. Perhaps Dillis could help her make a bathing suit?

James hailed Annie as he and Olivier dragged the boat clear of the waves.

'Hello there! Come and join us!'

Emma could sense Annie's uncertainty even from a distance, which somehow soothed her own shyness.

'Ho!' cried James again, waving now. 'Hello!' He marched across the beach towards her.

Annie Willard fiddled with the edges of her dress, tucking a stray strand of hair back up under her straw hat, only for it to slip down.

'Oh, hello,' she burst out. 'I'm sorry, but I have seen you coming past our cottage every day looking like you have so much fun, and today Mrs Elsworthy came to sit with Papa, so I had to come out and find you and I'm Annie and,' she put her hands to her mouth in horror, 'I'm talking too much.'

'Not at all, Annie,' said James, shaking her hand heartily. 'It's a pleasure to make your acquaintance. I'm James Linden. This is my sister, Emma. And this is our good friend, Olivier. Come and join us. Are you fond of boats?'

Annie's face was a mixture of astonishment and delight. She tucked the strand of hair up under her hat again and this time it stayed in place. 'I-I-I don't know. I've never had much to do with boats.'

'Well, there's no time like the present to find out. Come on.' James headed towards the water, calling over his shoulder. 'Emma is going to learn to swim. Can you swim, Annie?'

'Swim? Why no! Are you really going to learn to swim?' She looked at Emma in awe.

'Yes, I think I might. It shouldn't just be the boys who have fun.' The two girls laughed and linked arms as they strolled after James and Olivier, any trace of shyness swept aside. 'How long are you able to stay?' Emma asked. 'Will you have to get back to your father soon?'

'No.' Annie beamed. 'I can stay all afternoon if,' her face fell, "if that's all right with you?'

Emma squeezed her arm. 'Of course that's all right with us.'

Annie's face brightened. Emma knew from that moment she would grow to like her very much.

And she was right. That summer the four of them became thick as thieves.

Emma stopped mid-stride. 'Oh, I've forgotten my book!'

She knew where she'd left it, on the table in the hall. The excitement of trying out the new bathing suit, now draped over her arm, had pushed all else from her thoughts. 'You go on and meet Annie, she'll be waiting. I won't be a minute. I'll catch you up.'

Emma turned without pausing for a reply, and half-skipped, half-ran back up the lane to Kersbrook.

It was a glorious day. She smiled, remembering how Dillis's enthusiasm for making a swimming costume had surprised her.

'Too right, why shouldn't you swim?' she'd agreed.

Emma couldn't wait to try it. In her imagination, she would put the suit on, dive beneath the waves, and be transported to a prehistoric world where *ichthyosaurs* and great *plesiosaurs* swept past in jewel-like seas.

She was pulled up short from her reverie as she neared Kersbrook. A dark-haired figure, dogs milling at his feet, was leaning on the gate. Malcolm Greep.

Instantly, the day didn't seem quite so warm. She slowed, goosebumps prickling over her skin. Perhaps she would leave the book.

But he had seen her and part of her resented that he might make her change her plans, so she carried on, head held high. He straightened, but didn't move, blocking her path.

'Good afternoon, Miss Linden.' His tone was jovial, but his eyes were cold, assessing her like an animal caught in one of his traps.

'Good afternoon, Mr Greep. Could you please...?' Her voice trailed away as he slid his arm across the top of the gate, not opening it, but resting it there. She felt her face turn red and hot.

'It's a beautiful house, this.' His voice was casual as his gaze swept over Kersbrook. 'I had hopes to live here myself. Perhaps, I still shall.'

She swallowed hard. *What did he want?*

'Belonged to your mother's family, I understand. Sad she died so young. And no funeral, I heard?' His eyes narrowed on her, as if about to take aim with his gun.

What did he know about Mother's death? Emma swallowed again, her voice a whisper. 'If you please—'

'And your father passing in such tragic circumstances,' he continued, speaking over her, 'leaving you an... orphan, I suppose, is the correct term. If anything should happen to your brother, you would be alone and... unprotected. So sad.'

Emma tried to ignore the shivers running up and down her spine. 'I am not friendless, Mr Greep.'

'No? Friendships can be rather unreliable in my experience.' He paused. 'Do you know what I've been wondering, Miss Linden? Why you and your brother are still here. Why you haven't gone back to London.' He brought his face close to hers. She could smell tobacco on his breath, his stiff waxen moustache suddenly grotesque. Her heart thudded. 'Why a young man like your brother, an Oxford graduate no less, widely expected to take his place in the family businesses, is whiling his days away planting trees and paddling at the beach?' He shook his head, as if confused by an amusing riddle. 'Does that not strike you as odd, Miss Linden?'

When she didn't answer, he carried on. 'I like secrets, Miss Linden, especially when I discover what they are.'

Emma couldn't stop herself from shaking. Malcolm Greep suspected something was wrong with James. This was a threat. If it got out, they would have to leave Kersbrook and James would be admitted to an asylum.

'Emma!' They both turned at James's shout and the sound of his running feet.

The dogs barked ferociously.

'What's going on here?' he demanded, eyes fixed on Greep.

The gamekeeper looked James up and down. 'Just passing the time of day with your sister, Mister Linden.' He pushed open the gate. 'Making sure she gets safely home. You never know who's about in these quiet country lanes.'

Emma stepped quickly through, desperate to be away.

James took her arm as they hurried up the path. The front door safely shut behind them, he held her trembling hands in his. 'Did he harm you, Emma?'

She shook her head. She couldn't possibly tell him what Greep had said or hinted at – it would surely bring on another episode of James's illness.

'We were waiting and when you did not come...' He pulled her into a tight hug. 'I'm glad I came to look for you.'

They found her book on the table as she'd remembered. Walking back down the lane to the beach, Emma wondered how often Greep snooped around Kersbrook when they weren't there. She resolved to be extra careful and lock the doors in future.

*Kersbrook, Summer Holidays 2023*

The boat sent up a spray of water as we pushed off from the shore. We waded in after it, gasping at the cold.

'She floats!' cried Amin, jubilant.

I'll be honest, I wasn't sure she would. She was old, but we had worked hard, sanding and repainting her, even repairing a few holes, and had loads of fun too. Rosie named her 'Grace', after her gran, which she painted in gold letters on the prow.

'What do you think, Rosie?' I asked, leaping into the boat. It bobbed on the waves like an empty bottle in the bath.

She laughed. 'Good as new!'

'Ha!' yelled Amin. 'Better than new.'

Me, Rosie, Amin and Imogen had spent every

day together – I feel like I'll remember that summer for ever. Cooling off in the shade of the woods, going on long cycling expeditions down hidden green lanes, walking over the hill to the beach. We spent a lot of time there, swimming, fishing, fossil-hunting and eating ice cream. I actually got quite good at catching mackerel. We helped Naomi and Dan on the farm and played with Daisy in the hay meadows. I even had a go driving the tractor, ticking off a life goal I didn't know I had.

Amin turned thirteen on the 15th of August. It's hard to believe he's one of the youngest in our year, he's so tall. Imogen brought the drinks and crisps. Rosie made sandwiches, one for each of us. She must have checked with me a thousand times what his favourite filling was, she was so anxious to get it right. Chicken and mozzarella. It made me laugh because Rosie would never normally touch anything with meat in it. And I even had a go at baking a cake, which I smuggled to Kersbrook in my rucksack. Point is, we'd absolutely gone to town.

We found the perfect spot for our picnic on the shady edge of the garden, looking out over the fields.

Amin's face was magic when we brought it out. He never guessed for one minute. I even got some of those actually not-so-hilarious candles that won't blow out for the cake. And after Imogen had cycled carefully, so as not to make the coke fizz up when we opened the bottle, Amin shook it on purpose, shooting a spout of froth high in the air.

Imogen rolled her eyes.

Rosie shrugged and laughed. 'It's his birthday!'

'Too right! Got the rest of my life to be sensible!' He grinned. 'Now give me some of that cake.'

I ate so much food I felt like one of those roly-poly weeble toys that rolls about on its stomach. All I wanted was to sleep in the sun. But Amin was propped up on his elbows, looking at the view. I could tell he was hatching a plan.

'Y'know, we've not explored those woods. We should go there.' He pointed to a hill covered in trees, not far away.

'Yeah, why not,' I agreed lazily, though was quickly brought up short by Rosie's reaction. I don't know how the others didn't notice the tension coming off her.

'I don't fancy it,' she said slowly.

'Ah, come on, it'll be an adventure. We've been everywhere else. And it *is* my birthday...' He raised his eyebrows hopefully at her.

She didn't reply but I could see she wasn't happy.

'I'm always up for an adventure, but it'd be better another time.' I patted my stomach. 'I'm so stuffed I don't think I'll be able to move for the rest of the day.'

'Oh yeah, don't want you being sick like that time in primary school, remember?' Amin laughed as he turned to Imogen. 'Word to the wise, he is not good in the back of a minibus—'

Aware of Rosie sitting stiffly by my side, I butted in to keep the atmosphere light. 'Amin, if you say one more word, I promise I'm going to vomit over your head.'

We were laughing then, but I had half an eye on Rosie and was glad when I felt her relax.

We had one week left of the holidays and were coming back over the fields from the old mill when Amin stopped and pointed to the wooded hill.

'Right, today is the day. You can't put me off any longer. We are going to explore those woods *this* afternoon.' He said it grandly, as if he were announcing a polar expedition.

I glanced at Rosie, but couldn't catch her eye.

'I dunno,' I replied, peering at the dark shape of the hill. Perhaps she wasn't bothered after all, but there was something about it that spooked me.

'Uh-uh, wrong answer. Jude from Devon has just lost out on an all-inclusive holiday to Alicante.' Amin did his best impression of a TV game show host. 'Come on, let's go and have a look.' He was already striding off in that direction.

I tried again. 'Isn't it nearly lunch time?'

'Here, have a banana.' Imogen passed me one from her bag. Trust her to have a snack on board.

A single line of barbed wire circled the woods, held up by rotting wooden posts. Beyond that the trees grew thickly. This wasn't like any other wood we had explored that summer, where insects hovered in sunny spotlights through the leaves. It didn't seem that any light got in at all. It was deathly silent. No birds sang, no bugs whirred. No shuffle of a rabbit or badger. It was full of shadows.

'Looks too overgrown to walk through,' I said, trying not to sound pleased.

'Over here,' called Amin. 'There's some sort of path.' He ducked under the barbed wire and disappeared. Imogen and Rosie followed him. Grudgingly I went along. It was cold away from the sunlight, the trees pressing in. Our feet kicked up layers of thick, dry leaf mulch. No grass. No ferns. No wildflowers. Everything seemed dead. The path didn't go far, petering out at a big flat rock, half-buried in the soil. Beyond, the woods blocked our way with thickets of low-growing shrubs.

'The end of the line. Never mind,' I said.

Rosie suddenly sat down on the rock.

'You all right?' Imogen asked, sitting beside her.

Rosie scanned the undergrowth, frowning. 'Can't you feel it?'

'Feel what?' Imogen took her hand, concerned.

Rosie studied her face. 'Something bad.'

'Come on, let's go,' Imogen cut in, swapping a worried look with me.

Rosie nodded slowly, but it took a while before she would follow us back the way we'd come. I've never been so glad to get out of a place, ever.

We looked the woods up on one of the OS maps we found on the shelves at Kersbrook. It was called Holwell Woods, part of the Holwell Estate. Rosie already seemed to know.

'Yeah, those were the woods they were going to bulldoze for a new road. Do you remember? I brought a petition to school.'

I did remember. That felt like a lifetime ago.

Later that afternoon, I found her peering out of one of the windows on the upstairs landing.

'What are you up to, Rosie?' I asked.

'I've never noticed before,' she said, not looking at me, 'but you can see Holwell Woods from here.'

That place had really got under her skin.

I caught her at the window a handful of times over the next few days, staring out, lost in thought. Whenever I asked her about it, she shrugged it off, laughing. 'Just checking...'

But she never said what for.

**25**

*Kersbrook, Summer 1888*

Dillis proclaimed it a miracle and even Mr Kerr was impressed. That morning, Major Willard sat in regal splendour in a wheeled chair at the edge of the field, under the shade of the huge horse chestnut tree. His contorted figure was wrapped up in blankets despite the warmth of the summer's day. Annie explained that the apoplexy had left him vulnerable to the cold. Even though he couldn't speak, Emma could tell from the way his eyes sparkled that he was delighted to be there.

James and Olivier had insisted there must be a way for the Major to leave his bed. So they had set about building the chair themselves from odds and ends. It might not be the smartest carriage, but it had footplates and padded arm and headrests to support the Major's motionless limbs and leaning head. Then they heaved the chair up the lane and across the field, so the Major could follow the harvest.

'Major Willard, you are the master of the picnic and I expect you to alert us to anyone who tries to sample the supplies before the allotted time,' commanded James.

The lunch was packed away in baskets and placed in the deepest shade to keep it cool. James had baked late into the night to contribute to the harvesters' picnic that Dillis and the other women had prepared. Major Willard's eyes danced with merriment.

'Oh, you will take that duty very seriously, won't you, Papa?' said Annie, clapping her hands together.

'That includes you, too, James. Just because you made some of the food doesn't mean you get to creep up here when no one is looking,' joked Olivier.

James made a gesture of mock offense, then laughed.

'Come on, Mr Kerr has started,' Emma called to them.

Mr Kerr looked like a king, sitting up high on the reaper-binder, his wide-brimmed straw hat pulled low on his head. By his side, the sails of the machinery spun, cutting the golden dry wheat into sheaves and tossing them out for the harvesters following behind.

Harvest drew in everyone from the community. It was the job of the men to follow the reaper-binder, gathering four or five pairs of sheaves and jamming them upright into the stubble to make a stook. The women and children followed, picking up any leftover stalks, known as the gleanings. Annie and Emma worked companionably next to each other. It was hot and hard, but Emma felt contented, side by side with her friend. The heat beat back from the earth and she was grateful for the bonnet, keeping the sun off her face. Ahead of them, the horses pulling the machinery flicked flies away with their tails.

At last, Mr Kerr raised a shout and they gathered under the horse chestnut tree to share the picnic. Emma could hardly keep her eyes from James who was laughing and joking with the other young men.

She felt suddenly alarmed when his face darkened, the conversation turning serious. One of the young men was telling an upsetting story and she thought she read the name 'Malcolm Greep' on another of the men's lips. But James saw her looking, meeting her gaze with a warm smile, and the mood in the group lightened.

In the bright sunshine, the memory of how ill James had been in the winter, and even as recently as Easter, faded. He was so like his old self now. In that moment, she truly believed he would never be ill again; that she, Olivier and Kersbrook had healed him.

Because they had always returned to London by September, James and Emma had only heard of the wonder of the Harvest Home feast that the Kerrs threw for those who helped bring in the harvest. This year they would be able to taste it for themselves. Long tables laid out in the threshing barn sagged with meats, vegetables, puddings, tarts and ale. Swags and garlands of hedgerow greenery, flowers and ribbons hung from the rafters. Annie and Emma were crammed on a bench opposite James and Olivier. The space was full of jolly chatter. Emma drank it in.

'And when you were swimming and realised there was a jellyfish floating beside you,' tears poured from James's eyes, 'I've never seen anyone get out of the water so fast.'

'Oh, stop it. You don't much like them either.' Emma laughed. She couldn't quite believe she'd learned to swim.

'I thought you did very well to get out of the water so quickly with that bathing suit on.' Olivier was clutching his sides. 'It must weigh a ton when it's wet!'

It had been a wonderful summer.

Then, when the plates had been cleared and the cups replenished, Mr Kerr rose out of his chair, tapping the shoulders of two of the young men. One of them put a fiddle to his chin, the other strapped an accordion to his chest and Mr Kerr stood between, looking like a big old oak barrel in his brown suit. He hooked his thumbs into his braces, took a deep breath and began to sing:

> *'Come, my boys, come; come, my boys, come,*
> *And we'll merrily roar out Harvest Home!'*

The music swelled, filling the room with its infectious beat. By the chorus there wasn't a person in the room not on their feet, tapping their toes, clapping and joining in. James took hold of Emma's hand, spinning her round.

How life had changed in only one year. Emma caught his eye and knew he was thinking the same. As awful as James's illness had been, it had set them free. Neither would ever go back to the way they had lived before.

James was exhausted after the festivities, so Olivier and Emma walked Annie home, chatting contentedly. After seeing her safely inside, they strolled up the lane to Kersbrook, pausing at the gate before going into the house. The harvest moon was an enormous shining coin, resting on its edge on the darkening hillside. A skein of geese flew overhead, their wings beating out the rhythm – south, south, south. The seasons were turning and Olivier was leaving tomorrow.

'Emma, before I go, there's something I must mention.' His face was serious. 'I didn't want to spoil the fun of harvest by worrying you and James, and I really don't think it's anything to be anxious about.'

'What is it, Olivier?'

'It's more odd than anything. I received a letter from Mrs Carter. She was visited by a man asking questions about her time in service under your family. I'm sure it's nothing, but she was concerned as he seemed particularly interested in you and James. She gave him nothing and was proud of the fact.'

Emma's thoughts raced back to Greep's threats. 'Did she say what the man looked like?'

'No. Why? Do you know something?'

She studied his face. Dear, kind Olivier, who had worked so hard to bring them to safety. She couldn't add any more to his burden. No, she would keep her suspicions to herself. If it had been him, it sounded as though the gamekeeper hadn't discovered anything anyway.

She dodged his question. 'You must take some of James's blackberry jam with you. You know how he says clifftop blackberries taste the best.'

Olivier laughed. 'I'll think of Devon every time I spread it on my toast.'

Emma shook her head. 'I wish you didn't have to go.'

'I cannot say that the library at Oxford holds much appeal,' Olivier admitted. 'But summer's over, Emma, and you and James have settled so well. It was a risk, but our plan worked.'

'Your plan, Olivier. I don't know what we would have done without you.'

He smiled and they stood in silence for a moment before going inside, Emma forcing down the doubts surfacing in her mind. Would their plan work? James was well, but for how long? She thought of her mother's promise. *I will keep you safe.* Would it be enough?

*Devon, Autumn Term 2023*

That summer went by way too fast. Before we knew it, Rosie and I were standing at the school gates on the first day of the new school year.

'Everyone's staring at me,' she whispered, eyes large with panic.

'They're not,' I replied firmly.

'They are.'

'Really, they're not. Andrew Loney tried to dye his hair blue and ended up dyeing his face too. It's still not washed off. Everyone's staring at him, believe me.'

She gave me a small smile and we walked into school together.

**26**

*Kersbrook, Autumn 1888*

After the excitement of the Harvest Home feast and then Olivier's departure, life at Kersbrook settled into a steady pattern. James had gained strength over the summer. Now, as autumn fell, Emma listened to him work with Dillis in the kitchen, chatting and laughing as they mixed and baked. Physical activity seemed to bring peace to his mind and body.

Emma helped him dig over the vegetable garden, heaving piles of manure across from the farm. He chopped wood for the fire and they walked and walked for miles most days, all over the surrounding countryside. Along the beach and up over the cliffs, Emma on the lookout for fossils and special rocks, Mary Anning and her own research on the pebblebed never far from her mind.

They knew the place like the back of their hands. James would stride out with his long legs and Emma's orange scarf looped around his neck. He appeared absorbed, as if listening intently to some far-off drum beat, eyes fixed on the horizon. At times he seemed to forget Emma was with him and she would run to keep up. On two occasions they saw Malcolm Greep in the distance, dogs at his feet, gun cocked over his arm, but never again at Kersbrook.

Annie came to visit whenever she could, but Emma would usually go and sit with her. It was too cold for the Major to go out in his chair now, and it needed the strength of two men to get him into it. Olivier wrote often, sending Emma books and specimens to paint – shells, fossils, interesting stones, feathers, dried flowers. He had decided to change courses and would now be taking up medicine. Annie and Emma read his letters together. They had so many interests in common and devoured the books he sent, discussing them earnestly, Annie marvelling at Emma's paintings.

One day, in the parlour at the Willards', Annie leaned forward.

'Emma, we know a great deal about illness in this house. Please, will you tell me about James?'

Emma gazed into her friend's gentle eyes and knew it was safe. So she began with the day James's strange letter arrived at Old Brompton Road, full of plans for an outing to see a tiger.

The days grew shorter and colder as winter loomed. It was October and they'd been living at Kersbrook for almost a year. As dusk fell, Emma would sit at her desk in the dying light to paint, while James read. One evening, she looked up from her work and gazed out at the darkness creeping over the garden. A belt of trees now grew thickly all around it, though bare without their foliage. Outside, the occasional flying insect flickered against the windowpanes, attracted by Emma's lamp.

James was lying on the wooden-framed settee as usual, the colours of the cushions glowing bright in the lamplight, his head resting in the crook of one arm. But tonight, his book lay open on his lap. She watched him as he turned over his left hand, stretching his fingers and clenching them, his expression one of marvel and bewilderment.

Suddenly, he jumped to his feet, giving Emma such a fright that she nearly smudged her work. He announced he would go for a quick walk before bed.

'No need to trouble yourself, Em. Stay and finish your painting. I shan't be long,' he said, returning from the hallway with his jacket and scarf, before loping off into the gloom.

At ten o'clock, Emma stood up and stretched. She rinsed her paintbrush in the water pot and laid it down. In the kitchen, she warmed some milk for them both, but the clock ticked on and James did not return. By midnight, her second cup of milk finished, she could barely keep her eyes open. She stood at the conservatory door, scanning the darkness. Why was he not back? Her heartbeat thudded in a rush of panic. She placed her lamp on the sill. There was nothing to worry about, she told herself, he could look after himself. Still, she couldn't seem to stop trembling.

Next morning, she woke stiff and cold, wrapped in a blanket on the couch. She grimaced at the nasty crick in her neck. Blinking against the light, it took her a moment to remember where she was and why.

James!

She sat up, instantly awake.

And there he was, asleep, curled underneath her chair. His clothes and hair were dishevelled. Mud clogged the soles of his boots. A loose stitch in his orange scarf danced in the draught of his breath; on her desk, a sprig of holly, the red berries as bright as blood.

Emma tiptoed into the kitchen and filled her water pot, then carefully sat down, mindful not to disturb him. She picked up her paintbrush, dipping it into the water, pressing into the green pigment, and began to paint.

Things went on like this for some time, James striding out into the darkness by night, sleeping under her chair by day. Where did he go? Emma tried not to think about it. Tried not to think about the way his eyes flickered from point to point around the room as the evening drew near, as if watching the path of swooping birds. Or the agitated way he picked at the skin around his nails. It reminded her of how he'd behaved before Kersbrook had healed him. But he was different to the way he had been then: he didn't seem ill. They still talked together, he was attentive, not absent, as if in another world while in the same room. There was a decisiveness to him, like he had found a purpose and a peace in his night-time wanderings.

Emma was convinced he couldn't be staying out all night. Surely he came back after she went to bed. He would never leave her in the house alone until morning. Would he?

She often found herself running her fingertips over the words carved into Mother's desk.

*I will keep you safe.*

Then, one night, Emma made a decision. Before she could change her mind, she slipped through the conservatory door, across the cool grass to the outbuildings and found the chisel lying in a dark corner among the tools.

She resisted the urge to peek over her shoulder, as if her father might step out of the shadows and demand to know what she was doing. In the study, she faced the drawer and wedged the chisel into the gap.

The lock gave way with one heave, as if relieved to finally give up its secrets.

There was nothing much inside. Just a forgotten piece of stationery. She flicked back the flap of a folder, thin and insubstantial.

But there was something here after all.

The uppermost paper was a letter.

*London, 1866*

*Dear Mama,*

*Thank you for sending Papa's desk and chair. You were right, having them here has helped me feel more at home in London. When I touch the words carved into the leg, it feels like his promise to me – even though Papa told me they were old in his time.*

*I don't have many memories of India, but I do remember how he would sit at his desk and sketch the animals and birds that he saw in the mangrove forests for me. I remember his despair at the way the East India Company*

*carried on. I'm sure you're right and it was
this that led to the troubles he had before he
disappeared.*

*Just as you wrote it would be, the ammonite
was in the drawer – the one Papa found on
the beach as a boy. He told me once how the
Hindus make a pilgrimage to the mountain
temples in Nepal and bring back ammonites
found by the river. They call them Shaligrams.
and believe they symbolise Vishnu, god of
protection. I think that's beautiful.*

*I have news that will delight you. Charles
and I are expecting a baby. I am quite well so
you mustn't fuss. Deep down, I am certain it is
a boy. And if he is, I shall name him James.*

*With all my love,*

*Marianne*

Mother's *own* handwriting. Emma blinked away
tears. It was as close as she would ever be to hearing
her voice. It was like catching a favourite melody
she didn't know she'd forgotten.

Beneath the letter was another piece of paper, a
short, scribbled note:

*Dear Charles,*

*I implore you again, do not have Marianne admitted to that place. Send her to me. This house has always been a sanctuary for those who need it, I have never forgiven myself for not bringing John back in time. Here at Kersbrook, she will be well.*

*Lizzie*

Lizzie, Emma's grandmother, begging her father to allow her to care for Marianne in Devon. There was one last letter:

*Kersbrook, 1871*

*Dear Charles,*

*I'm glad to answer your questions. The nurse who travelled with her was full of compassion, but Marianne was so weak when she arrived. When I wrote to you, I thought she was regaining her strength.*

*On that last evening, we sat together in the*

*conservatory, watching the sun go down over the garden. She fell asleep in my arms and did not wake up.*

*You must not blame yourself. You thought the asylum was the best place and you had the children to consider. I'm grateful you allowed her home to me.*

*She was at peace at Kersbrook.*

*Take care of James and Emma, Charles. Bring them back here as often as you can. Keep them safe.*

*Lizzie*

Mrs Carter had been wrong. Mother didn't die in an asylum. Relief flooded through Emma. But Marianne had been very unwell. And so had John Hayes by the sounds of things. Her grandfather had loved to sketch the wild things around him, like Emma did. Then James. It was history repeating itself, over and over, like the spiral of the ammonite, round and round.

Emma walked slowly to the conservatory. The ammonite lay on her desk, her grandfather's desk, beside her tin of paints. She picked it up, now understanding why it had brought her such reassurance. And the promise in the desk leg, not a promise from Marianne but one *to* her.

No, not just for Marianne. As Emma traced the ripples and bubbles in the old glass panes of the conservatory, she felt it was just as much a promise from the house itself. *I will keep you safe.*

She considered the letters. What should she do? Tell James what she had discovered? She couldn't bear keeping secrets from him. He had a right to read their mother's words and to know the truth. But to learn that she had been so unwell? She couldn't do it. At least not now. She would wait for a better moment.

Emma retraced her steps to the study. She placed the documents in the drawer and closed it softly. The lock had opened easily, there was no sign of damage from the outside. No one need ever know it had been disturbed.

Emma woke to rain clattering against her bedroom window, the thin light of a wintery dawn tinting the sky. Had James returned safely? The question spun in her mind.

Wrapped in her blanket, Emma crept downstairs and peeked into the conservatory.

No James. Her lamp still burned on the sill.

Suddenly, there was a flicker of orange in the garden. She muffled a cry, following the flashing motion between the shadows. Some*thing* was out there. Something she couldn't make out. A fox? No, bigger. As big as a tiger. And James, somewhere out there too! She strained to see where the creature had gone.

Footsteps crunched in the autumn leaves and she stepped back into the doorway, nervous of confronting him. James wrenched at the handle, his breathing laboured as if he had been running. He bent down and turned out the lamp. His clothes were filthy, as though he'd been crawling through mud, his fingernails caked with it. He stretched his back as if trying to ease out a pain, then strode towards the desk, throwing himself in a heap under the chair.

She rubbed her neck, a headache blooming at the base of her skull. Half-dreaming and beside herself with worry, she'd imagined a creature in the grounds. What she'd taken for some great hunting animal had been James, running through the trees, running home, the orange his scarf. What a fool to

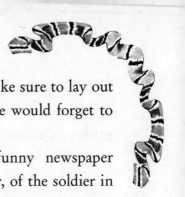

take such a fright. She would make sure to lay out some clean clothes for him or he would forget to change.

It brought to mind that funny newspaper clipping James had once sent her, of the soldier in India who thought he had turned into a tiger.

Such a strange story.

But it didn't answer her question: what *was* James doing out there like that, all night in the dark?

'Miss Emma, this has got to stop,' said Dillis, heaving a brace of pheasants on to the kitchen tabletop one morning in December.

Emma signalled to her to keep her voice down, but she would have none of it.

'You tell him, enough is enough. He won't listen to me.'

'I don't understand…' A sick feeling filled Emma's stomach.

'Every night, Miss Emma, every night someone around about here gets pheasants or rabbits left on their doorstep. Doctor Gregory opened his door to find a whole deer. Just lying there! Goodness knows how he did it. We've had more than our fair share at the farm. Don't tell me you don't know anything about it.'

'I—'

'Don't get me wrong, we're grateful,' she carried on. 'There's plenty of folks around here struggle to put food on the table over winter what with rents going up, but he's risking too much.' Dillis's face was taut with emotion. 'I'm sure Mister James thinks it's a very fine joke getting one up on Malcolm Greep, but he doesn't know what sort of man he's crossing.'

'James? Malcolm Greep? Dillis, I know nothing of this.'

'For a time, I thought he was poaching on the Holwell Estate, but the way I hear it, it's much worse. He's emptying the gamekeepers' snares and traps before they get there. Pinching what they've caught from under their noses! Carrying on like Robin Hood he is, taking from the rich and giving it away. Greep's put men out on watch but no one can catch him at it. They say he must be a ghost. But that's where he goes to of a night. Surely you knew?'

James's empty bed. His muddy boots. Leaves in his hair. Of course, it made perfect sense. But why would James purposely antagonise a proud, nasty man like Malcolm Greep? A man determined to discover the truth of James's illness. Determined to expose it to the world so he can have Kersbrook for himself!

'You tell him, Miss Emma, it has to stop or he is going to be in more bother than he knows. Malcolm Greep will not be crossed.'

## 27

*Kersbrook, December 1888*

The day was cold and damp, the kind that seeps into your bones and is impossible to thaw unless you're sitting almost on top of the fire. The furrows between the ridges in the fields were full of water, reflecting grey sky above. Afterwards, Emma couldn't help but feel that James had engineered their meeting with Malcolm Greep that afternoon. She now knew that Greep was more than just a proud, nasty man – he was cruel and he was dangerous.

What Dillis refused to tell, Emma found out through village gossip. The trumped up charges he made against anyone he took a disliking to, to get them evicted from Lord Holwell's land. The bribes he used at every opportunity. The gunshot wound he inflicted on young Harry Pym when he strayed into Holwell Woods. Everyone knew about the brandy Malcolm Greep gifted to the local Chief Inspector, so that he turned a deaf ear to any rumours that reached him. Emma tried to tell James how Greep had threatened to expose them should he discover the truth of James's illness, but it only seemed to make things worse.

'Yes, yes – he's a horrid man. I know!' was all James would say.

'Where are we going?' she called after her brother that morning. He marched ahead, orange scarf streaming behind. He was following a route across the fields that Emma had never taken before. She hadn't really wanted to come out at all. Olivier had sent another parcel with a beautiful shell inside which she was itching to paint.

'Come on, Emma, just up and about, here and there. We'll be home for tea, I promise.'

He was jumpy and excitable. Occasionally he would pause, as if listening to directions from an unseen companion, nod, then forge ahead. She trudged through the mud, hoping the physical activity would soothe him. The hem of her skirts was sodden, weighing her down. She cursed a leak in her boot, a loud squelch accompanying each step. She wished she was at home. The only other life they saw that day were crowds of crows, rising and falling across the skyline like a widow's veil. She trudged on, desperately trying to match James's pace.

Emma's unhappiness deepened when the distinctive shape of Holwell Woods veered up ahead. Though the trees were bare, they grew so thickly that it appeared a dark impenetrable mass.

'James, I am not going into those woods.' Emma stood, slowly sinking in the mud. 'I will not,' she said, the tremor in her voice betraying her exhaustion.

He walked back and took her hand. 'Dearest Em, I promise we are not going into the woods. We will not set one foot on Lord Holwell's land. But please, I would like to go a little further. Will you come?'

'James, I want to go home. I am cold and wet and Olivier sent me a conch shell to draw.'

'Just a little further, Em,' he insisted.

'Very well.'

They followed the line of a hedgerow along the edge of a field. Suddenly there was a break in the hedge and a tall figure loomed, his dogs letting rip a volley of barks. Malcolm Greep looked as shocked to see them as Emma was to see him – they hadn't been up close since that encounter outside Kersbrook. James didn't seem at all surprised.

'Mr Greep, a pleasure to see you,' he said cheerfully.

Greep's dogs growled, hackles raised.

'You!' He spat.

'Now, now, there's no need for bad manners.' James was actually teasing him and looked like he was enjoying himself heartily. 'We're not trespassing. This hedgerow is the boundary of the Holwell Estate. You hold no authority over my sister and I, since we're on this side.'

Malcolm Greep's eyes fixed on James.

'I know your secret,' he snarled. 'I have learned what you really are.'

Emma was horrified. How could Greep know?

But James just squared his shoulders and glared at the gamekeeper, his voice suddenly threatening. 'In that case, you should be more careful how you treat people…'

Emma couldn't believe the change that had come over her brother.

Malcolm Greep took a step backwards, eyes widening. Something had passed between them that she did not understand.

James turned to her, his tone light again. 'Well, it was delightful chatting, but we must get on. Emma has a conch to draw. Goodbye, dear Mr Greep!'

He swaggered away, leaving Emma to run after him, the baying of the dogs ringing in her ears.

She splashed through muddy puddles to catch up.

'James, *are* you stealing from Lord Holwell's estate? This time you must answer me. Dillis showed me the pheasants you left on her doorstep.'

There was no slowing his stride. He grinned at her over his shoulder, a mischievous glint in his eyes.

'James, you mustn't. Malcolm Greep is a horrible man. Dangerous. Why must you provoke him? James, we could lose everything...'

But he carried on.

'James Linden, I am not going one step further until you tell me where you go at night. Promise me you are not going on the Holwell Estate.'

She could hardly hold back the tears. Greep might have forgotten them, forgotten his desire for

Kersbrook. But now he would be even more hungry for revenge. The thought of what might happen to James if the truth came out, after everything they had been through, was too much.

'Promise me.'

At last James paused, his shoulders sagging.

'Don't you see? I can't help it, Emma, it's my nature. I'm protecting you all. Guarding you. Keeping you safe. Besides, he'll never leave us alone.'

*Protecting us all?* She stared into her brother's eyes, beginning to follow his thinking. So James was inspired by some misguided sense of justice. Did he imagine each stolen pheasant was a punishment for the sorrows Greep inflicted on the community? Each act of trespass a poke in the eye for Greep snooping into their affairs?

'Keeping us safe? Do you mean like the stoat or Bhayankar Raaja or the tiger king, Rai Bagh, protecting their territory?'

His face lit up. 'Yes! Oh, Em, you remember and you understand! There's more to the world than most people realise, but you see it! This place,' he swung his arms wide, indicating the countryside around him, 'and the people who live here are mine to protect from the likes of Greep. I'm not the only one with a secret he would use against me. It's up to me to challenge him. And I'm glad to do it. It's a place of such wonder and beauty. Let me show you—' He delved into his coat pocket with both hands, cupping them gently, as if worried he would crush the thing he held.

'Look...' His voice was hushed as he raised his palms to her. 'Look at the golden hue of the wings. And the size of it! I've only seen pictures of butterflies like this in the tropics. And there's more, up in the woods, a whole jungle full of miracles.'

Emma nodded, unable to speak. This was no golden butterfly.

Nestled in his hands, James held a large, yellow leaf.

*Devon, December 2023*

Rosie changed during that school term, so slowly I didn't notice at first. Mental health is tricky like that, it's not like you can see the blood from a cut. It started the day we went to Holwell Woods

– something about it disturbed her. She became sort of blank, the way people look when they've run a marathon and need Lucozade, but also touchy at the same time.

One break time, I came out of French and found her standing at the top of the stairs, head on one side, as if listening for a sound that was hard to make out. I don't know how long she'd been there. No one seemed to notice, they just pushed past her, the usual rush to meet mates or pick up food from the canteen before the bell went.

I looked around the stairwell. Thankfully Zak and his minions hadn't clocked her. They'd given her a wide berth after Mr Tucker, the headteacher, gave our year group a stern talking to about Rosie coming back to school and the counsellor had delivered a presentation on mental illness.

I made my way up the stairs. 'Hey, Rosie, you all right?'

No answer. She looked tired and sort of dishevelled.

'Rosie, everything okay?'

I took hold of her hand, my heart pounding. I was back on the high street, standing on the bench.

She turned sharply, frowning at me, and wrenched her hand away.

'Yeah, course I'm all right. You're crowding me, Jude. I'm all right.'


*Kersbrook, December 1888*

In his letters, Olivier congratulated Emma on finding a way of talking about James's condition. A tiger – an excellent metaphor for the complexity of his affliction. The truth was, she was paralysed, and at a loss as to how to help her brother.

In the late afternoon light, Emma walked with him, his thick paw pads crunching the last of the autumn leaves. The colours of his golden coat mingled with the colours of the trees. Then, in the deep dusk, their paths would fork. Emma walked back towards the house, closing the door carefully behind her, but never locking it. And he would turn and be gone, a flash of orange, into the night.

Olivier sent her a pendant on a shimmering silver chain. The pendant showed Saint Blaise, the patron saint of wild animals. One day, he promised, he would take her to India and they would see real tigers. Emma sighed and left a lamp on the sill to guide her tiger home.

**28**

*Devon, December 2023*

The winter that year was the coldest since 1987. Northerly winds and polar lows brought snowy weather and temperatures hitting a low of -17.6 degrees. On the 19th of December, when the snow started falling, somewhere between registration and physics, Rosie disappeared.

She had definitely been there at registration. Definitely.

I passed Imogen in the corridor. 'Hey, have you seen Rosie?'

'No, why? She had physics, didn't she?'

'Yeah, only I was meant to meet her outside the lab to walk to English. Probably, it's nothing.' I shrugged. 'Bet she's gone ahead.' I didn't want to stress Imogen out, but Rosie always met me on time – a sick feeling swelled in the pit of my stomach.

'Hey, mate.' Amin bounded up behind me. 'Hi, Imogen.' He cast a gleeful look over his shoulder, then leaned in and whispered, 'News is... the weather is turning bad and they're thinking of letting us go early. Two words for you... Snow. Day!'

'Mmm, well until they say otherwise, I've got to get to geography.' Imogen shot me a strained look as she turned to leave.

'Imogen! If they let us go, meet at the main gate. We'll go sledging!' Amin shouted after her. He looked at me. 'She doesn't like snow?'

'We haven't seen Rosie since registration.'

'Ah.' He pulled himself up straight, face serious.

'I've got a bad feeling, Amin. I've tried ringing her but her phone's off.'

'Simmons! Dridi!' a teacher called down the corridor. 'Move it! You've got classes to get to.'

'On our way, sir!' Amin called back. He slung his arm around my shoulder. 'I bet she's fine, mate. Doesn't she have Mr McClusky for physics? He makes everyone turn their phones off in class. She'll be sat there waiting for us in English.'

But she wasn't. Rosie's seat by the window was emptier than Mum's purse before payday. Outside, the snow fell thickly. I threw my bag onto the desk. Where was she? The sick feeling rose in my throat. I yanked out my books and sat down, flicking open my copy of *Jane Eyre* by Charlotte Brontë. Mum watches period dramas all the time. There's lines in Jane Austen that make me laugh out loud. But though they're both Janes, they don't have much in common.

*Jane Eyre* is one messed up book.

Amin doesn't really do angry, but he got properly angry over it. He finished it before the rest of us and kept going on about it, so I carried on reading and eventually caught up. It was the character of Bertha that most upset him. When he found out Bertha was mixed ethnicity it hit a nerve and he went back through every bit about her.

The hero of the book, Mr Rochester, keeps his mad wife, Bertha, in the attic. Just say that to yourself like it was happening today: *Man keeps wife with mental health problems prisoner in the attic.*

And then it's all lovey-dovey at the end. After Bertha dies, Jane Eyre marries Mr Rochester. Amin reckoned Mr Rochester didn't deserve a happy ending and should have gone to prison for a *very* long time.

The day of the snowstorm, we were studying the bit where Jane runs away from Mr Rochester. It goes like this:

*Not a tie holds me to human society at this moment – not a charm or hope calls me where my fellow-creatures are – none that saw me would have a kind thought or good wish for me. I have no relative but the universal mother, Nature: I will seek her breast and ask repose.*

*I struck straight into the heath; I held on to a hollow I saw deeply furrowing the brown moorside; I waded knee-deep in its dark growth.*

Suddenly I knew exactly where Rosie was.


*Kersbrook, January 1889*

'Look, Em, it's snowing.' James stood at the window.

The winter that year was the coldest since 1836. A great blizzard brought more than two feet of snow. Temperatures plunged to a low of 21.7 Fahrenheit at Bury St Edmunds in Suffolk. Convicts from Dartmoor Prison were forced to dig out warders from their snowbound homes so they could report for duty.

It was late afternoon when James and Emma noticed the first flurry. They watched in silence as the swirling flakes slowly but surely made the familiar world strange.

The snow came thick and fast as the evening drew on. James sat, unable to keep his eyes from it, whispering under his breath, as if sharing his wonder with an invisible child at his side.

Emma couldn't make out his words. She was used to this symptom of his illness and it bothered her less than it had done. He stood up now and again, to open and shut the conservatory door, so it wouldn't become blocked.

As night fell, the flakes took the place of stars, reflecting back Emma's lamplight.

'I'm going to warm some milk before bed,' she said at last. 'Would you like a cup?'

'Mmm.' James didn't take his eyes from the snow.

Emma padded off to the kitchen, warming herself by the stove as the milk heated through.

Standing with a mug in each hand, she felt the blast of cold air from the open door in the conservatory before she registered James's empty seat.

She gently closed the door and placed the lamp on the sill. Even on a night like this...

He couldn't help it. It wasn't his fault. But she felt frantic. Something told her that this night, of all nights, she should have found some way to keep him home.

Next morning, she stood in the freezing conservatory, bare feet turned to blocks of ice, staring at the space under her chair. James was not there.

In the end, it was fury that drove Emma to dress, pulling on her heavy coat, wrenching on her boots. She was furious with James that he had not come home, furious with the snow that covered everything and furious with the universe that this... this *affliction* should fall to her and her family. Her fury powered her out into the lane, shovel in hand, calling and shouting for James. Her voice sounded pitifully small, its force sucked up by banks of snow.

Emma's calls brought Dillis and Mr Kerr outside, their coats flapping. No, they hadn't seen James. Where on earth could he be? Dillis and Emma exchanged looks, two words hovering between them like a curse. Holwell Woods.

'Try the Willards',' suggested Dillis. 'Perhaps something happened to the Major and he went to their aid in the night. We'll search the farm. Maybe he took shelter in one of the outbuildings. We'll find him, Miss Emma.'

Emma shook her head, her fury giving way to despair. She knew they would not find James at the Willards'.

Annie came to the door when Emma knocked, her face full of concern.

'No, we haven't seen him. Wait, I'll get my coat. Mrs Elsworthy has just arrived to see we were all right in the snow. She won't mind sitting with Papa while I help you search.'

Grateful for Annie's kindness, Emma could only nod and stamp the cold from her feet as Annie disappeared into the house. Moments later she was by Emma's side, trudging back up the lane.

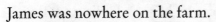

James was nowhere on the farm.

'I've looked everywhere m'dear.' Mr Kerr pressed his great palm on her shoulder.

Emma covered her face with her hands.

'I'm going to round up the lads. He must be lying injured somewhere, perhaps trapped by the snow or fallen on ice,' he said.

Dillis nodded, waiting until he was out of earshot before taking Emma and Annie's hands in a steely grip.

'Come now, girls, whatever mischief that boy of ours has got into, we're going to bring him home.'

The going was slow and tortuous. The brightness of the snow made Emma's eyes water. While her upper half sweated, her toes were frozen solid. All was silent across the white fields, not a creature stirred, not a single set of tracks marked the pristine snow. Dillis led the charge, muttering to herself. Emma briefly caught some of the words. Dillis was praying. Desperately praying.

**29**

*Devon, December 2023*

*'Not a tie holds me to human society... I waded knee-deep in its dark growth...'*

I was out of my chair like a shot, convinced I knew where Rosie was and that she was in danger.

'Mrs Wright, Mrs Wright.' I ran to her desk. 'Please, Mrs Wright. I'm sure something has happened to Rosie Linden. She skipped physics and she's not here either. I reckon I know where she is. Please can I go?'

Mrs Wright looked at me over her glasses. 'Sit down, Jude. You're not going anywhere until that bell rings.'

I felt my chest was about to explode. 'Please. You don't understand,' I begged.

She was the worst teacher to appeal to. Mrs Wright absolutely loves a rule. 'Sit down, Ju—'

Out of nowhere, the school bell rang. Everyone stared at each other. It wasn't time for the end of lesson yet.

The class erupted. The Head was sending us home. Amin had been right.

'Calm down, everyone.' Mrs Wright stood up, shouting over the cheering kids.

A hand grabbed my arm and there was Amin.

'Come on, mate. Now's our chance. Let's go and find Rosie.'

I nodded, struggling to get my phone out of my pocket as we bundled for the door. If we were going to Kersbrook in the middle of a severe weather warning, we needed help.

Imogen was waiting for us at the main gate.

'This is ridiculous!' She pointed to the snow laying thickly on her hat. 'Did you find Rosie?'

I shook my head. 'No, and I can't explain why, but I think she's gone to Kersbrook and I think it's really important that we find her. Fast.'

Imogen looked at me like I was stupid.

'Jude, Rosie could be *anywhere* and you want to go to Kersbrook on the off-chance. How would she have got there? How are *we* going to get there?

We can't cycle in this. We should be ringing the police.'

'The police will be busy dealing with the fallout from the snow.' I took a deep breath. I felt calmer than I had all morning. I had a plan. My thoughts fled back to that day on the high street. Rosie hadn't needed a police cordon or a hospital bursting at the seams; she'd needed people who cared for her. 'We're Rosie's friends. We're going to get her,' I said firmly.

Imogen sighed but Amin gave me one of his weird slapping hugs. 'Well said, mate. Well said.'

'We need to go. Alice is meeting us on Walden Road.'

'Alice? The paramedic?' stammered Imogen.

'Yes! Come on!'

It'd been a stretch phoning Alice, but I couldn't think of anyone else. There was no way I was calling Maddy. We'd ring her once we'd found Rosie and had good news. Alice's voice had been groggy when she answered and it was hard to talk while jogging down the corridor to meet Imogen. But when she heard Rosie had gone missing, she was instantly awake and promised she'd help.

I don't know what car I imagined Alice would drive, but it wasn't the battered four-wheel-drive pick-up truck she turned up in, with a bumper sticker that said *I'm not your darling* and a radiator that sounded like it needed a strong course of antibiotics.

'Get in and on the way, you can ring your parents,' she called, leaning over to open the passenger door. Me, Imogen and Amin wedged ourselves onto the broad bench seat and pulled out our phones.

Mum picked up after one ring. 'Jude? Where are you? The school sent a text saying they're closing for the weather.'

'Mum, I can't explain now, but Rosie's gone missing and we think we know where to find her and...' It tumbled out, like rubbish after a seagull's pecked at a bin bag.

'All right, Jude,' Mum said at last. 'But I'm going to call the police and I'll ring Maddy. And Jude... Once you get to Kersbrook, don't try to come home. Stay there and keep warm.'

'Okay, Mum. Gotta go.'

'Wait, Jude...'

'Mum?'

'Say a big thank you to Alice for helping.'

'Will do.'

'And Jude…'

'I've got to go, Mum!'

'I'm very proud of you, Jude, you know that?'

'Yes, Mum.' Seriously, how can you bask in a rare moment of the-boy's-done-good praise when you're on a rescue mission? I'd have asked for a raise on my pocket money if I'd had time to think.

On the radio there were reports of gritters stuck behind stranded cars, a petrol tanker jack-knifed in icy slush, closed runways at the airport. As we drove out of town, we passed abandoned vehicles and the flashing lights of police cars and ambulances. It was like something from an alien invasion film.

'Looks like I'm going to have a busy shift tonight,' muttered Alice, peering through the small triangle of windscreen. 'That's if I get back to base…'

As the roads dwindled to country lanes, we barely saw a soul. Snowflakes flickered in the truck's headlights. Drifts banked up against the hedgerows and a thick blanket smothered the fields.

Snowploughs hadn't made it out this far yet. I bit my nails. It was agony how slow we were going. Now and again the tyres slid and spun, but Alice quickly recovered. I was beyond grateful we had a professional ambulance driver at the wheel. The engine chugged away and the radio fizzed – a brief blare of David Bowie's 'Space Oddity' between half snatches of voices – but otherwise the snow fell silently, matched by the silence in the cab. We were willing the truck on, willing Rosie to be safe.

Kersbrook looked more enchanted than ever, the redness of the brick walls warm and welcoming in the whiteness. If I'd been ill like Rosie, I'd have headed here. Our feet sank deep in the drifts that billowed across the steps and up the path to the porch door. Imogen gave me a hard stare as we waded towards the house, which told me without words that I had better be right. It didn't look promising. The snow was smooth, not a footprint to be seen. The house was deserted. But I had never expected to find Rosie inside.

We couldn't open the porch door, so Alice brought two shovels from her pick-up and we set to work clearing the snow. Behind the frosty glass, Naomi had taken away the red flowers and replaced them with pots of bulbs we'd helped plant with little Daisy in October. The surface of the pots were bare, the bulbs snug beneath the earth. Only humans were daft enough to be out in this weather.

At last, the porch door grated across the snow. I rubbed my hands together to warm my numb fingers before trying the front door handle. My tummy flipflopped when it opened. Either Naomi was here, or Rosie was. No one else had a key.

I headed straight for the conservatory guessing what I'd find. Alice, Amin and Imogen's voices echoed around the rooms. The beachcombings cluttering the windowsills were like souvenirs from another planet. Shells, pebbles, driftwood and sea glass. Summer beach days seemed light years away from this silent, freezing world. The icy blast hit me as soon as I stepped into the conservatory, the door to the garden had been left wide open.

'She's not in the house!' I yelled, my heart

pounding, my suspicions confirmed. After reading that bit in *Jane Eyre*, I'd been sure Rosie's illness had returned. And remembering how sensitive she'd been about it in the summer, something told me she'd gone to Holwell Woods. When I saw the open door, I was certain. I ran into the garden.

The snow was shallow between the sheltering prongs of Kersbrook, but it soon became much deeper. I ploughed on, my legs already soaking.

Wiping flakes from my eyes, I saw the others crossing the terrace.

'She's gone to the woods. Holwell Woods. I know it! This way!'

'Jude, come back!' Alice cried. 'Jude!'

Pushing through the snowdrifts that covered the garden, I can't really say what I was thinking, but Zak Riley's taunt jumped into my head. *'You're her knight in shining armour.'* Was I trying to be a hero? The thought made me squirm. And if I found Rosie, what exactly was I going to do? Scoop her up like a Marvel Comic character?

'Jude!' Amin's voice called out. 'We're going round to the farm to see if Dan'll take us on the tractor. Come back, mate!'

I saw Amin waving his ridiculous spade hands at me.

But I had to keep going. I didn't want to save Rosie, as if she'd let me anyway. I just wanted to find her so she'd know we cared. Even if all I could do was sit with her until help came.

'Meet you at Holwell Woods!' I yelled.

'Jude!' I heard Alice shout, then Amin reply, 'You won't change his mind. Come on, let's find Dan.'

Not wanting to waste a second, I was soon beyond the boundary of Kersbrook. It was hard going, trudging across the frozen fields, frantically running scenarios in my head. What would I do if she was hurt? She'd be sure to be hungry. If only I'd thought to bring something for her to eat. The flakes continued to fall, the only sound the crunch of compacting snow under my shoes.

The snow had smoothed out every ridge and hollow so that I had no idea where it dipped until I was thigh-high in a drift, floundering around like I was swimming. Heart thudding, I gritted my teeth and hauled my way out. Holwell Woods was in sight.

Suddenly there was a flicker of orange between the bare trees, a flashing motion. I stopped, scanning the wood, my breathing hot and sore. An animal? A fox? No, something far bigger, far faster. I squinted...

It was Rosie!

Her orange scarf burning bright like a Belisha beacon against the white of the snow.

'Rosie!' I shouted, running now, but she'd vanished.

Desperate not to lose her, I lurched into the tangled undergrowth, but thorny branches like razor wire rose up, ripping at my clothes and scratching my hands. Holwell Woods were as thick and impenetrable as ever. I gritted my teeth, determined to ignore the spine-shiver that whispered at me... Was the wood trying to keep me out?

I circled the perimeter, searching for the path we'd found in the summer. It had to be here somewhere, but everything looked so different in the snow.

At last, I found it, a thin trail curving inwards. I ran, feet sliding from under me, gasping for breath, forcing my screaming muscles to respond, all the time scanning for a sign of Rosie.

And then she was there, in front of me, in the clearing with the flat rock. I skidded to a stop, chest heaving.

'I can't find him,' she sobbed. 'I've been searching but he's disappeared—' She dropped to her knees, hair falling over her face.

I kneeled beside her. 'It's okay, Rosie. Whoever it is, we can find them.' I touched her hand – it was ice cold. Her palms and the ends of her fingers were scratched raw. What had she been doing?

She looked at me. 'Jude, I think he's gone.'

I had no idea what she was talking about, but she recognised me, which was good. She was shivering violently, her lips dark purple, the skin around her mouth blue. I didn't need Mum to tell me this was what hypothermia looked like. Rosie needed warming up. All I had was my stupid school blazer, but it would have to do. Shrugging it off, I draped it over her and wrapped my arms around her. I would have to apologise later for giving her the grossest, sweatiest hug in the world.

Sitting there, willing warmth into her, felt like an eternity. I closed my eyes, straining for the sound of rescue. When I finally heard the rumble of an engine and the clunk of gears shifting, I thought I'd imagined it. My mind raced. Who would have come with Dan in the tractor? Most likely Alice. But would they know the path into the woods?

'Rosie, help's coming, but I need to show them the way.' I carefully eased myself away from her. She didn't reply. I was so stiff I had to brace myself against the rock, but couldn't help pulling my hand back in surprise. I'd felt something.

Half-hidden by lichen, the edges softened by weather, the carved spiral was as plain as day. An exact replica of Rosie's gran's ammonite, etched into the rock.

# 30

Alice never made it to her night shift. I felt bad
for the people she could have helped. But as she
said later, she might as well have been helping
Rosie as anyone else. And Rosie was in a state. She
was blue with cold, her school uniform torn and
heavy with wet, as Dan and Alice carried her
inside the house.

Amin was tasked with keeping Daisy happy
while Naomi hunted out blankets and hot water
bottles. Dan went to boil the kettle.

'Sit with Rosie and hold her hand,' I instructed
Imogen as I kneeled down to make the fire. I was
so frozen I could hardly make my fingers work.
She had gone all weird and useless, sort of wafting
about and flapping her arms. 'Take her hand,
Imogen.' But still she stood there, just staring
at Rosie.

Behind us, Alice was having low and urgent phone conversations with the crisis team and the duty psychiatrist.

Finally, Imogen whispered, 'I've never seen her like this. I didn't know this is what it was like.'

Rosie sat huddled on the sofa, her head in her lap.

I didn't reply. Definitely best not to share what was going through my mind. It was so many kinds of wrong talking over Rosie, as if she'd turned into a purple alien with two heads and couldn't understand English any more. I got that Imogen felt scared, but still…

'She could have died out there in the snow if we hadn't found her.' Imogen came to stand beside me. I passed her a sheet of newspaper to roll for the fire. I don't think she realised how close it had been.

'The thing I don't get is…' Imogen looked down at the newspaper. I mimed what she had to do. 'The thing that doesn't make sense, is the timing.'

I pushed my roll into the wood burner and impatiently held out my hand for hers. I was desperate for warmth.

'Rosie left school after registration. We realised she'd gone after physics, so that's about an hour. By the time we got out of school, you could add on another half an hour. It took us three hours to get out here by *car...*'

'Come on, spit it out, Imogen.' I held a lit match to the edges of the newspaper, trying to stifle my irritation. Rosie was sick, what did timings have to do with it?

'Rosie only had an hour and a half head start on us. Jude, how does a thirteen-year-old girl get over here that quickly – by foot, in the middle of a snowstorm? And is *then* found in Holwell Woods. It doesn't make sense.'

I slammed the door shut on the burner with satisfaction as the roaring flames from the newspaper caught the kindling and started to blaze.

'I dunno, Imogen, maybe someone gave her a lift? Maybe I'm wrong and she didn't come to the house first. We found her and that's the main thing, right?'

Suddenly I felt exhausted. Imogen might have a point, but I wasn't sure where she was going with it. I had no energy left. I felt like I might cry.

'Hmm,' she nodded slowly. 'I still don't get it. To cover so much ground...'

I sighed. It had been a tough day for all of us. 'Imogen, until we can look inside Rosie's head and experience what she's experienced, we're never going to get it.' I knew that wasn't what she meant, but it seemed a ridiculous thing to be talking about.

Luckily for Imogen, Naomi came back then with bundles of blankets and Dan arrived bearing a tray with mugs full of tea. I went and sat beside Rosie, but her eyes were closed, lips moving. I leaned into her a little, shoulder touching shoulder, so she'd know I was there. I didn't want to frighten her. Just anchor her. Here. With us.

*Kersbrook, February 2024*

Rosie didn't go home straight away. Instead, Maddy moved into Kersbrook, and as it was too dark to cycle over after school, I didn't see much of Rosie that Christmas.

One Saturday, I leaned my bike against the pebble wall outside the house and leaped up the steps. There were new shoots over the bare trees and in among the grass, daffodils were coming out.

Rosie sat on the old wooden-framed couch in the conservatory, surrounded by cushions.

'Tea, Jude?' called Maddy.

'Just some water, thanks.' I sat down beside Rosie.

'Nice to see you,' she said, smiling faintly. They'd tweaked her medication and she was still getting to grips with it.

'You too. You look good.'

'Do I? I don't feel it. Let's not talk about that though. Any news from school?'

'Andrew Loney stuck a paperclip in one of the sockets in the physics lab and switched it on. It blew the electrics in the whole block.'

'Oh no!' She laughed.

'And Zak Riley's in love.'

'Zak Riley?!' Rosie's eyes nearly popped out of her head.

'Yep. A nice year seven called Sophie Massen. Amin reckons she'll be the making of him.' Amin says such grown-up things sometimes. I was just glad Zak'd stopped being mean. Though he was definitely punching above his weight.

Maddy came in and put my glass of water on the table.

'Thanks.' When she'd gone, I asked, 'How's it going, being here with just your mum?'

Rosie looked thoughtful. 'Really good actually. We've talked about loads of things we'd never talked about before. I guess it hasn't been the two of us like this since, well... I can't remember when...'

I nodded, but there was a lot about what had happened that I didn't understand.

She smiled. 'You look worried, Jude.'

'Me? No, it just sounds heavy going.'

'Yeah, I guess it's been difficult *and* good. We've talked quite a bit about Gran and about the family.'

Rosie clasped her hands in her lap. 'You know that photo of Gran in the hall? Well, she had a brother who died quite young, Mum's Uncle Tom. I knew he existed, but no one ever spoke about him. It was like he was the black sheep of the family. Mum wonders now if he had the same thing I've got. Apparently, Gran went to stay with him for a while when Mum was around my age. We wondered if he'd been sick and they stayed together here to help him get better?'

She paused, checking for my reaction.

'Wow,' was the only word I could think of.

'Right, wow.'

'Do you think that was when the photo was taken?' The mysteries in Rosie's family were starting to make sense.

'It would tie in. Grandad must have known about Uncle Tom's illness, and maybe people did guess, but turned a blind eye. Mum said a lot of that went on when she was growing up. You didn't interfere in other people's private business and mental illness was something to keep hidden. Naomi says she has a vague memory of Uncle Tom from when she was little and her mum and dad ran the farm. But we won't ever know for definite.' She paused again. 'It's helped knowing it affected someone else. Someone in my family. And that Kersbrook might've been a safe place for him, just like Naomi said it was meant to be.'

And then she smiled properly, right up to her eyes. 'Me and Mum made a promise to each other that it can't be a secret any more. We have to talk about it. So, yeah, it has been really good.'

I looked at my feet. 'I wish you'd talked to me and Amin and Imogen. I wish you'd told us about feeling ill.' It made me sad that she hadn't felt able to confide in us. 'We might have been able to help, that's all.'

She nodded. 'It wasn't because I didn't trust you. It came on so gradually, I didn't even notice at first and then I was scared. But you're right, I should have said something.' She smiled again. 'Thanks for coming for me, by the way.'

We sat there in silence. She looked so calm, but I was a tangle of emotions. I had stuff I needed to ask her.

'Rosie? Holwell Woods.' I felt like I was throwing a grenade. 'There was something about them when Amin pointed them out on his birthday. I'm right, aren't I? It wasn't just about the petition, was it? Did you find something out about the accident? Was that it? Did something happen in those woods?'

She didn't answer straight away. When she did, there were tears in her eyes.

'Nothing definite. Just a creepy feeling to start with. And then I read about some local rumours, which would have been during the time Emma Linden lived here, but that's all they were, rumours that something bad had happened. After we went there, I began to get paranoid and then the voice started – calling, crying out. Everywhere I went, I could hear this voice. Someone was in the woods, in pain. And I—' She stopped suddenly as if afraid to go on.

'And you—?'

She winced at the memory. 'And I was the tiger, keeping everyone safe. Someone in my territory needed help. On the day of the snowstorm, something weird seemed to happen to time and it wasn't daylight any more, it was night time. I followed the voice and I found a man in the woods, a young man. He was injured somehow, scared and alone. I stayed with him until dawn came, keeping him warm. And the woods were magical, filled with huge golden butterflies. Then it was daylight again and I couldn't find him. I searched but... he'd gone.'

*Kersbrook, January 1889*

The dark shape of Holwell Woods was capped with white. Annie, Dillis and Emma crossed onto the Holwell Estate at the gap in the hedge. They didn't have far to go to find James. He was lying on his back under the trees, next to a low, flat rock, eyes closed, breathing ragged. His arms were clutched to his side, a red streak staining the snow. Emma fell on her knees beside him. There was no time for words. The baying of Malcolm Greep's dogs carried through the icy air. They had to move.

'This is a gunshot wound. Malcolm Greep shot James last night. He's coming back for him in the daylight, isn't he?' Annie's eyes were wide with horror.

Dillis put her hand on Annie's arm. 'No more talk, lover. We need our strength to shift this boy. Come now.'

They heaved James up, Dillis on one side and Emma on the other. James groaned, but didn't resist. Annie unwound the scarf from his neck and held it to his side to staunch the bleeding. Tears streamed down Emma's cheeks. He mustn't die, certainly not here on Holwell land. With each step she repeated to herself: he mustn't die, he mustn't die, he mustn't die...

She never knew how they made it out of the woods, the howling of the dogs hot on their heels. Her chest was on fire as they reached the gap in the

hedge. The silhouette of Kersbrook was just visible. She locked eyes with Dillis over James's drooping head, knowing they would not stop until they got him to safety. What they both would have given to carry the burden of his illness for him over the past year. But now they would at least carry him home.

At last, in the distance, the familiar figures of Mr Kerr and the other farm workers spotted them. Strong arms lifted James. Annie, Dillis and Emma held hands as they trudged behind.

As they crossed into the grounds of Kersbrook, threading their way between James's trees, a hollow, sick feeling made Emma cry out. The men stopped in their tracks and she ran to her brother. Pulling James into her lap, she held his face in her hands and knew that he had gone.

31

She couldn't believe it. He could not be gone. He could not. She pushed her hot forehead against his.

Finally, Mr Kerr and his men carried James inside. After being helped into the house and sitting down on the couch in the conservatory, Dillis washed her face with a warm flannel.

Emma remembered little after that. Time blurred. Numb to the core, the world went on in shadow. People spoke above and around her like distant stars, their voices a far-off hum. And all the while she spun alone in the darkness.

*Kersbrook, February 1889*

James wasn't buried until the end of February. The ground was hard as iron and couldn't be broken until a thaw. Seven long weeks passed and the funeral was to be held in the little churchyard in the village.

Of the Linden family, only Uncle Henry came. His chauffeur waited in the great black car, ready to whisk him back to London as soon as his duties were performed. He behaved with stately solemnity, but Emma saw the relief in his eyes. A liability had been removed. Much to Emma's shock, Kersbrook now belonged to her. On Marianne's death, Lizzie Hayes had left the house to her grandchildren, held in trust by their father. It had taken Mr Grant some time to untangle, but in reality, it had never been within Uncle Henry's power to sell. James's shares in the business would pass to him but, as he declared pompously, he would see Emma was provided for.

Emma couldn't begin to think why Lord Holwell was there. She felt him watching her, his expression pained. She had never seen him up close, only once or twice, stepping out of his carriage in the village. He was a tall man and in his top hat he was even more of a towering figure.

After the ceremony, Lord Holwell waited at a polite distance while local people clasped her hand. They spoke kindly of James's generosity and his joyous spirit, but she heard them whisper among themselves of how thin and pale Miss Emma looked.

'Miss Linden. May I beg a moment with you? In private.' Lord Holwell's voice was clipped. 'It's a delicate matter.'

The three of them exchanged glances, Annie slipping her hand into Emma's, as Emma stammered, 'Annie and Olivier are my dearest friends. They will keep a confidence.'

'Very well.' His voice was low as he drew them to one side. 'I felt I must speak to you and I understood you were not receiving visitors. You already know that your brother was not the only person to be injured in my woods that night.'

Emma nodded. Malcolm Greep had tripped, knocking his head on a tree root. Doctor Gregory said his death would have been instant. The dogs had not been in pursuit of Dillis, Annie and Emma. They had been howling at the side of their fallen master, not far from where James lay.

'Nothing can be proved. But I cannot ignore the coincidence of the two men so close to each other, one dying from a gunshot wound and the other holding,' he whispered, 'a gun.'

She looked at him sharply.

Lord Holwell lowered his gaze. 'I do not want a fuss, but I believe I may owe you a debt.' He drew a notebook from his pocket, scribbling hurriedly in it. She watched him, confused. Debt?

'I have set up a stipend in your name, a significant sum of money, and I would be most gratified if you would draw on it whenever you have need.' He ripped the page from the notebook, handing it to her. 'Speak to my man of law about it. He will explain the details.'

She stared at the paper.

'Miss Linden.' His pained expression returned. 'I assure you that I will be more careful in my choice of employee in the future.'

She studied his face, struggling to understand his meaning.

Tucking his notebook into his pocket, Lord Holwell bowed and marched crisply away.

It was a dismal spring that year. Cold and wet. But Emma was glad, glad to wake to day after day of

277

damp, grey weather. It was as though the seasons themselves were acknowledging James's death.

April brought further grief with the passing of Major Willard. The endless damp started a cough, then a chill, and at last, pneumonia. Annie, in a state of shock, and adrift without the routine of meeting his needs, moved to Kersbrook, unable to be alone.

Olivier visited briefly for the funeral, his head crammed with anatomy and physiology for his exams, but at last, in June, he came for the summer.

'Do you see him?' asked Emma, eyes flicking over the carriage windows as the slowing train rattled into the station.

'Yes, there!' cried Annie and they ran to meet him.

As he stepped down onto the platform, James's absence, as real as his presence in life, hit Emma like a blow. She dug her nails fiercely into her palms to stop herself from crying. It would be just the three of them from now on.

To Emma, the following week was agony. The friendship between the four of them had always been so natural, but the oil greasing the wheels of easy chatter and laughter had dried up. Though they filled their days with activity, everything they did, everywhere they went, was brimful with memories of James. Yet they could not speak of him.

And Emma did not want it to be this way – the time they spent together permanently clouded with sadness. James would have hated it. But she felt unable to break the spell hanging over them.

At last, it was Annie who burst into the conservatory one morning, announcing, 'I can't bear this. Both of you, come on, we're going to the cliffs.' And she turned on her heel, marching through the house without waiting for a reply, reminding Emma a great deal of Dillis.

Stumbling after her, Olivier and Emma exchanged curious looks, and for the first time since his arrival, they both smiled.

Clambering up the steep cliff path behind Annie, Emma could not help studying her friend in wonder. She strode out in the sunshine, head held high, loose tendrils of hair bouncing in the breeze. There was something different about her. When had this change happened?

At the top, they stood together on the springy grass, gazing out towards the horizon. The air was warm, the sea perfectly still, gulls hovered on the thermals just off the cliff edge. Emma inhaled deeply.

'It's strange to think we were picking blackberries here, only last summer,' said Olivier slowly. 'It seems a lifetime ago.'

Annie nodded. 'James wanted to make jam.'

Blood rushed in Emma's ears. She felt the very earth must have gasped at the mention of his name.

'You remember how it took days to get the kitchen clean again?' Annie turned to Emma and Olivier, a challenge in her eyes. *Let's break the spell*, she seemed to be saying, *I dare you to remember him out loud.*

Emma began in a whisper. 'He always said these clifftop berries were the best, but I think he wanted an excuse to see the view.' Her gaze slid from Annie's relieved smile to the glistening water, shielding her eyes from the sun. Her skirts billowed with the breeze. She felt light enough to take off and soar like the gulls.

'Perhaps they taste sweeter *because* of the view,' said Olivier, and he laughed. It was good to hear him.

'Just recently I haven't been able to stop thinking of James that first day I met you on the beach,' said Annie, 'busy grasping life, though he was so ill. I feel as if I have been old before my time, worn down with cares and now I only want to be young and free.' Suddenly she threw her arms out wide as if she might embrace the sky. 'I want to grasp life too!'

Emma smiled. 'How are you going to grasp life, Annie? What are you going to do?'

'Take up hot-air ballooning?' suggested Olivier.

Annie laughed. 'No, nothing so extreme. I've been wondering about training to be a teacher. Mister Combes is due to retire. I thought, perhaps, if Emma would come with me to ask him, I might speak to Lord Holwell about holding the position for me.' She blushed, suddenly embarrassed and anxious for Emma's opinion. 'What do you think? I've always wanted to be a teacher but with Papa's condition it never seemed possible.'

'Oh, Annie!' Emma wrapped her arms around her friend. 'I think that's a marvellous idea. Truly. You'll make a tremendous teacher.'

'Now your turn,' urged Annie. 'Emma, Olivier, what are you going to do to grasp life?'

Olivier looked thoughtful. 'Well, I shall complete my studies, but… I did wonder about ordering some daffodils from Lucombe's and planting them under the trees at Kersbrook… to remember James…' He looked uncertainly at Emma. 'If you don't mind, that is?'

Emma beamed at him. 'Another marvellous idea.'

'We could plant them before we both leave at the end of summer,' cried Annie.

'And you, Emma?' Olivier's question was hesitant and she found herself hesitating too. A clump of yarrow caught her eye in the grasses at her feet. She bent down and picked a sprig, twirling the stalk. Was she really ready to live again?

As she gazed at the cluster of tiny white flowers, thoughts blossomed in Emma's mind. She could help on the farm. Dillis would be happy to have another pair of hands. She could pick apples for the cider-making, even if she couldn't bake an apple cake as well as James. And there would be pickling and bottling to do from the vegetable patch – James's vegetable patch. She could paint and read. Perhaps write that paper she'd been planning, on her theory of the Devon pebblebed. Emma took a deep breath. Yes, she would repeat the work she and James had done together, walk the paths they had walked. And in each dig of the spade, each streak of paint, each written word, and each stride across the fields, she would be in step with him. She knew she would always find him in the rhythms of the landscape, the community and the earth he loved.

Emma took hold of Olivier and Annie's hands, smiling. 'Well, I shall have to make trips to Oxford, and wherever you go to study, Annie, but mostly,' she gazed back out over the sea, 'mostly I will be here.'

## 32

*Kersbrook, September 2024*

All the windows of the house were open. It was a dimpsy evening. Dimpsy is a Devon word for a soft warm evening with a greeny, golden light. Rosie was in one of the attic bedrooms. There's a dressing table by the window in that room, with a mirror and a hair brush on top. A drawer was open and Rosie was standing, looking down at something.

She didn't hear me come in and for a moment, I panicked. I'm often like that now. I won't ever forget the feeling when I realised she'd gone missing that snowy day. I'm always a bit watchful that she might go again and I won't be able to find her.

'Rosie?'

She turned and looked at me with clear eyes. Not gone. Still here. She was smiling.

'I found these. Look, Jude.'

She held a wodge of old photographs.

The images were black and white and edged with a border. A young woman appeared in all the photos, wearing long dark skirts and blouses buttoned up to her neck. Strands of hair had come loose from her bun and curled around her face. In some of the photos there was also a young man with neat hair slicked over, leaving a precise side parting. Something about his eyes seemed kind. He obviously liked her because his hand rested on her waist. Women in saris, tall men in tunics and turbans and elephants laden with saddlebags jostled against a backdrop of jungle foliage.

'Oh,' Rosie frowned at a headshot of the woman, 'she's wearing my gran's necklace, look. The one of Saint Blaise.' Her hand flew to her neck where the pendant hung.

'I wonder who they are. They seem so happy.' Something about the pictures sent a tingle up my spine.

I read the sloping handwriting on the back of

the photograph. *Gwalior, India.* I thought of that poster of the Bengal tiger in Rosie's room.

'Do you think they saw tigers?'

Rosie gave me a look. 'Stop it. You're not funny.'

'No! I wasn't even thinking that. Not you and the tiger thing. Honest.' I did my best embarrassed I'm-an-idiot, forgive-me smile.

She rolled her eyes and showed me a tiny rectangle of a photograph. 'Look at this one.'

I could just make them out in the grainy image, standing on the steps of a stone building. He was wearing a dark suit and her hair was hidden by a lacy veil. Smiling beside them, another young woman in a flowery hat was throwing rice in the air. On the back, in the same sloping handwriting, were the words:

*Emma and Olivier, 1899.*

'No!' Rosie exclaimed. 'Emma Linden! My great-great-grandmother. I can't believe that's really her. Wait a minute...' She paused. 'That paper about the pebblebed was written by someone called Olivier Falconet. It can't be a coincidence. I bet we can find out!'

She looked out of the window, the setting sun lighting up her face. I thought of how she'd always dreamed of travelling.

'Yeah, and we should go to India and see tigers.'

'Will you stop it with the tigers!'

'I'm serious.'

'What? Instead of going to school tomorrow?' she said teasingly. Tomorrow was her first day back since her second illness.

'No, course not tomorrow. I mean, in the future.' It seemed like a genius idea. How cool would that be?

Rosie looked at me. 'I'm just going to try and get through tomorrow. Finishing school is something I can't imagine at the moment.'

I could see her point.

'All right then. I'll do you a deal,' I said, putting my hand out and doing my best impression of Mr Harris. 'You get through tomorrow, and the day after that, and the day after that, and we'll go to India when we finish school.'

She laughed. 'You really believe I'll be all right, don't you, Jude?'

'Course.'

'Okay then.' She shook my hand. 'It's a deal.'

**33**

*Kersbrook, September 2027*

It's funny to read this journal from when I was thirteen. I wrote about what happened so we wouldn't forget. As if we ever could. Maybe our story will help someone else in the future. Rosie was adamant there should be no more secrets.

Today I'm back at Kersbrook after another amazing summer. Me, Rosie, Amin and Imogen are sixteen. Imogen and Amin are together now. It took them forever to realise they liked each other, so it was a relief when they finally admitted it. Looking into my crystal ball, I don't see them ever being apart. Amin is starting his plumbing apprenticeship with Rosie's stepdad, Rob. Imogen has plans to study to be a physiotherapist. I hope I'm right and they do stay together. If nothing else, their children will be phenomenal at triathlon.

It took me a long time to get used to calling Mr Harris, Pete. He and my mum are really happy. Even though she's got someone else to hug, I still get my obligatory thirty seconds every morning.

What about Rosie? She's the queen of clean living and the healthiest person I know. She drinks two litres of water every day. She cycles everywhere and I've never seen anyone eat so much fruit and veg. She's strict about getting enough sleep. It's never not going to be a struggle, but she works hard at being well. She had another relapse about six months ago when she forgot to take her tablets. We were at Kersbrook and, thankfully, she was only missing for one night. Now she has injections and it's much better. She's still passionate about protecting the planet. She recently spoke at a meeting of the County Council about stopping a housing estate being built on the site of an endangered bat roost – she'd been helping a campaign group with the bat surveys. I've heard so much about it, even I'm getting excited about bats. Did you know female greater horseshoe bats give birth upside down and catch their babies with their wings? Seriously, the housing estate should be shelved on that fact alone.

Rosie's got plans to study zoology at university. She was inspired by her great-great-grandmother, Emma Linden. We found out lots about Emma after discovering those old photographs.

She married Olivier Falconet, but she never took his last name. Olivier was the man who published the paper on the Devon pebblebeds, though Rosie and I have a theory about that. He was Rosie's great-great-grandfather and he was quite a special man in the world of medicine. There's loads about him online. He was a psychiatrist and a campaigner for the rights of the mentally ill. He pioneered compassionate care for children and young people showing early signs of psychosis. One of the world's good guys. But he wasn't known for his love of geology.

No, it's Emma's paintings and drawings of rocks and fossils that fill the walls of Kersbrook. In those days, it was hard for women to study. Oxford University didn't give proper degrees to women and academic journals wouldn't publish papers by women. It was Mary Anning all over again. But Rosie reckons Olivier might have submitted the paper with his name so Emma could see her work

in print. She left us a clue too, a little ink drawing of an ammonite fossil, right at the end. Like Emma was signing her name.

And that was the symbol I found carved into the rock at Holwell Woods. We went back there and it was a different place. The barbed wire was gone and the trees had been thinned out. The sun shone and grass grew where before there'd been no life. It was like a cloud had been lifted.

We found out that Emma's brother, James, died in an accident in Holwell Woods. It was nearly impossible to uncover anything else about it. But we knew he had been in his early twenties and his gravestone is in the churchyard in the village near Kersbrook.

We talked a few times about what Rosie thought she'd seen in the woods that time in the snowstorm. But there was no way of making sense of it, so we left it at that.

We also discovered that the woman in the hat in the wedding photograph was Emma and Olivier's best friend, Annie Willard. She was the teacher at the village school near Kersbrook, and apparently the kids loved her. The last day of the summer term

is still called 'Miss Willard's Day', that's how loved she was. The whole school heads down to the beach for ice cream and paddling.

Rosie and I have vowed that we will go to India when we're eighteen. That was the deal we made. We've planned everything. For the final part of the trip, we're going to the Siju Wildlife Sanctuary in the Garo Hills, where there are *real* tigers. Rosie wants to research Garo folklore about a king who could turn into a tiger. She says some people reckon 'tiger transformation' is a traditional way of understanding mental illness. Rosie won't fly because of the climate crisis so we're getting the train. We travel to London, then get the Eurotunnel to Paris and from there, all the way through to Iran, Pakistan and on to India. It's going to be a massive adventure. Mum's having kittens, but she'll come round. She's got time to get used to the idea.

On this last evening of the school holidays at Kersbrook, I'm in the bedroom overlooking the garden. I can't tell you what makes me open the drawer in the dressing table, but I do. There's the white edge of a piece of paper poking up. It must have slipped between the side and the bottom of the drawer. I hook it out with my finger. It's a pencil drawing of a tiger and it's incredible.

Rosie comes in and looks over my shoulder. 'Wow, what a beautiful picture. It's like one of Emma's drawings. Isn't this where we found those old photos of Emma and Olivier's trip to Gwalior? So they did see tigers! Amazing to have got so near to be able to capture it like that. Can you imagine if we see one?' She smiles and walks away.

I look more closely. It's a majestic animal, so proud. The evening light highlights its whiskers, its eyes glowing. The tiger is lying on a rug underneath a chair. The legs of a table cross the drawing in verticals. The carved pattern inlaid with droplets of mother of pearl feels familiar. And I'm sure I recognise the design on the rug. Suddenly I realise where I've seen it before.

Downstairs in the conservatory.

The image lodges like a lightning bolt in my chest. A tiger? A real tiger here at Kersbrook? And James, the brother who died young and tragically. Had he been sick like Rosie and her Uncle Tom? There's a tiny, faded date in the corner of the paper. 1888. Eleven years before Emma and Olivier married and went to India. Possibilities rearrange themselves in my mind.

I remember the flicker of orange between the trees that day in the snowy woods. Something far bigger, far faster than a girl. And how *had* she got over to Kersbrook so quickly the morning of the snowstorm?

I lay the picture carefully back in the drawer, shaking my head, and follow Rosie out of the room. It's just a drawing. People don't turn into tigers. Not actual, real tigers.

Though Rosie'd always be a sort of tiger to me – brave, kind and courageous, wanting to keep us all safe.

# Acknowledgements

First to those who inspired this story. I can't name you and you may never know. Thank you.

This book has been like a fossil itself, embedded deep in the cliff. I am eternally grateful to fellow-excavators, my wise, long-suffering agent, Lindsey Fraser, and my brilliant, thoughtful editor, Lauren Atherton. To the Zephyr team, thank you for your enthusiasm and for putting your vast talents behind this book. Thank you for giving me the opportunity to develop and grow as a published author, and to bring a second novel to readers.

I would like to thank the myriad people who have taught me about land, personhood, place and dignity. As Wendell Berry so perfectly conveys in the quote at the beginning of this book, we are connected in ways not often recognised by everyone.

Prime of all these connections is the one with the soil beneath our feet. It makes us who we are, from the nutrients in our food to our sense of place in the world. Thank you to the landworkers I have been privileged to know, who taught me history can be read in landscape and showed me how the earth resonates with the experiences of the people who live in it. Chief among them is my dad, who is yet to meet a boundary he didn't immediately breach.

To my mum, who taught me how to see the poetry even when the hills were not safe.

To SCBWI friends, in particular, Clare, Emma, Jenny, Katina, Amanda, and Kay. Thank you for rolling through the highs and lows of the author journey with me. Special thanks to Emma, who gave me a nudge at just the right moment, and to Jenny, whose intervention stopped Tiger being confined to the bin.

To Sarah Broadley, Emma Perry and now Bruna De Luca at *My Book Corner*; Louisa at *Roaring Reads*; *Imagined Things*, *Bookbag*, *Owl & Pyramid* independent bookshops; and *Exeter St Thomas Library*, who have been unfailingly kind from that first day when I threw a little book into the abyss and felt like I might fall in too. To all in St Thomas, the best, most-supportive community in the world.

To Gemma and Linda, for cheering me on.

To Molly for giving this book a clinical check-up. To Avisha and Sonali for correcting my Hindi. Mistakes are very much my own!

My littlies – inquisitive, kind, loving and so funny. You make every day sparkle.

To Tess – as you have grown, I have grown up. Thank you for your big-heartedness, your sincerity and your patience.

And finally, to you the reader. Most of all, I hope you will find Tiger a beautiful story about the human spirit. Take care of your friends. Ask them if they're okay. You don't need to be able to fix it, just notice, and support them to find help when they need it.

# A  Q&A on mental health
# with Hannah Foley

**Why is it important to tell stories about mental illness?**

We find it *really* difficult to talk about mental illness in the UK. 30% of people say they would not feel comfortable talking to a friend or family member about a mental health diagnosis and 50% would not feel comfortable talking to an employer. That's a big problem. It stops people with a mental illness getting the help they need. And negative attitudes make the experience of a mental illness much worse. Throughout history, humans have used stories to ask difficult questions where cold hard facts might have made everyone run away and hide behind a cushion. Stories bring us closer to different experiences. We begin to empathise with another person's situation, asking what it might feel like to be in their shoes. When we do that, we look beyond our own fearful feelings, recognise someone else's needs and change our behaviour. Stories transform that *scary person over there* into *our friend who needs kindness over here*.

## How was mental illness viewed in the Victorian times?

The Victorians had a variety of theories about the causes of mental illness, from infected teeth, immoral behaviour and not going to the toilet often enough. No one yet understood the difference between mental illness, emotional distress, learning disabilities and a whole range of physical causes of confusion. Alexander Fleming didn't discover penicillin until 1928 so a nasty infection could easily see you labelled as mad. There were very limited treatment options too, so people tended to get locked away when no one knew what else to do.

The image of the Victorian asylum inmate in chains comes from the beginning of the 19th century. By the middle of the century, more compassionate methods inspired by a group of Yorkshire Quakers were being used. These involved good food, rest and access to fresh air in green surroundings. But towards the end of the Victorian era, the sheer number of patients being admitted to asylums had overwhelmed the system. Patients were restrained, locked in padded cells and given strong drugs to make them cooperative.

We have a much better understanding of the biological processes behind mental illness now which has helped improve attitudes. Nobody would see mental illness as a moral failing today and we don't lock people up in manacles. The honesty of high-profile celebrities about their mental health difficulties has opened up national discussions. However, ideas from the Victorian times continue to hang around: it's surprising how often newspaper headlines, pop songs or TV storylines rely on Victorian images of mental illness. We are certainly more compassionate, but we still have a long way to go.

## Why does stigma still exist today?

Sadly, there is still a lot of stigma around mental health. Studies have shown that though we're more accepting of mental health problems like anxiety and depression, most people continue to find illnesses such as schizophrenia frightening and confusing. These attitudes spill over into the way we treat people with mental illness. Nine out of ten people with mental health problems say that stigma and discrimination have a negative effect on their lives. It's easy to feel overwhelmed when we read statistics like that, but it's important to remember change begins with us. By being comfortable discussing mental wellbeing and treating people with mental illnesses with respect, we will challenge the thoughts and behaviour of the people around us. It would be wonderful if we could talk as straightforwardly about experiencing an episode of psychosis as we do about a heart attack.

## Can empathy help?

Empathy is about putting yourself in someone else's shoes. If you can imagine another person's feelings, you can start to understand their behaviour and it can change how you respond to them. It surprises me how often being frightened looks like being angry. If you are ever in doubt, be kind.

Sometimes, even though we can empathise, a person's behaviour can be scary and confusing or we might feel worried and afraid by the way other people are responding to them. If you feel unsafe, it's important to remember, it's okay to remove yourself from the situation and get help.

## Do nature and physical activity impact our wellbeing?

Exercise is brilliant for wellbeing. Researchers have shown exercise reduces anxiety, depression and negative mood by increasing self-esteem and cognitive function (our ability to think well). It's thought that exercise increases the blood circulation to our brains and improves motivation, mood and our response to stress via a part of our brains called the hypothalamic-pituitary-adrenal axis.

Being in nature has also been shown to be great for our mental health. Researchers found that being near trees, hearing birdsong and seeing the sky improved mental wellbeing for several hours after the experience. It was especially good for people who were at high-risk of developing a mental illness.

It's important to say that the opposite has also been shown. Researchers use the term 'aesthetic stress' for the way a degraded physical environment can affect people's mental health. We know that poorer neighbourhoods are more likely to be affected by mental illness, where people often have less access to nature and green spaces

**Has your work as a nurse inspired this story?**

In one of my jobs, I worked as a District Nurse where I visited people in their homes. I used to see a number of people who had mental illnesses. Some of these people were very elderly and had never had any formal diagnosis or support from mental health services, often out of fear and shame. They and their families had managed their symptoms, living quiet and dignified lives, all the time hiding a deep secret. I also visited younger people with mental illnesses who lived in supported living and I learned so much from them about the daily work of being well and the assumptions I'd made about what health looks like. Though none of the details of my patients' stories appear in James's and Rosie's, the spirit of their stories very much does.

## The pandemic had a negative impact on people's mental health. What can we do to keep well?

In British culture we tend to separate our minds from our bodies and treat them as if they're not connected. In sport, people talk about having to push their body and when they're sick, people talk of it being like their body has let them down. But they aren't really separate at all and the things we do for our physical health help us have good mental health too.

Eating a healthy, balanced diet, drinking plenty of water and exercising regularly helps our minds and bodies to be strong and have more energy. Sleep is important for allowing our bodies to repair. We only release growth hormones when we sleep at night and our brains do important emotional processing during a phase of sleep called REM. Having a variety of interests and getting out in nature are good for us too.

Sometimes sad or worrying things happen and we can't avoid that. Then it's helpful for our mental health to have people we can trust to talk to. Researchers call this a good social network. It doesn't matter who's in your social network, whether it's family, friends, a youth worker, a dance teacher or sports coach. We all need some help to process tricky feelings at times.

## How can we support a friend who is struggling with their mental health?

The biggest thing is to notice. You know your friends so you'll be best placed to see if there's anything wrong. Perhaps, they've been quiet and withdrawn. Maybe they seem very tired or have been neglecting their appearance by not brushing their hair or putting on clean clothes.

You could begin by asking them if everything's okay and mention they don't seem their usual selves. It's good to find a quiet time and comfortable place to ask these sorts of questions. Try to empathise with their answers by putting yourself in their shoes and remember to be kind. What sort of things would you want someone to say to you if you were in their position?

Just because you notice, doesn't mean you have to be able to fix it. In fact, you almost certainly won't be able to. Raise your concerns about your friend with a trusted adult. Young Minds have a useful list of the qualities to look for in a trusted adult:

Open-minded, patient, comforting, observant, reliable, supportive, big-hearted and committed.

**You can read more about this here:**

https://www.youngminds.org.uk/media/kkllkxbi/
what-makes-an-adult-someone-to-turn-to-about-
your-mental-health.pdf

**Useful links:**

www.youngminds.org.uk

www.place2be.org.uk

www.annafreud.org

www.mind.org.uk/information-support/
for-children-and-young-people/useful-contacts/

# Who was Mary Anning?

Mary Anning was born in 1799 in a town called Lyme Regis, in the South of England. This is on a special bit of coastline, called the Jurassic Coast, where lots of fossils can be found. Mary's family were very poor. Out of nine children, only Mary and one of her brothers survived to be adults. Mary didn't have the chance to go to school, but she could read, and taught herself geology and anatomy. Her father, Richard, was an amateur fossil-collector and he would take Mary out to find fossils with him.

When she was twelve, Mary found a strange skull and then the outline of a long skeleton. No one knew what it was. The word 'dinosaur' hadn't been invented yet, much less '*ichthyosaur*'! Mary knew that scouring the cliffs after a storm was the perfect time to find fossils and she would go out with her

little dog, Tray, even though it was dangerous. Later on, she was the first to find a complete *plesiosaur* skeleton.

Mary's father died in 1810 and she started selling her fossils to tourists to support her family. She came to the attention of eminent scientists who would often buy her fossils and write academic papers about them, but not give her any credit. The Geological Society of London refused to let her be a member. In fact, no women were allowed to be members until 1904. But the problem wasn't just that Mary was a woman. She was working-class and a religious dissenter. It's hard to imagine now how much power the church had in people's lives at that time. Many dissenters believed we should be able to ask questions and not just be told what to do and think by a priest.

Mary continued to be poor throughout her life. She died of breast cancer when she was only forty-seven. But, as Emma says in this book, she really did change the course of science. Through her fossils, she showed that species had become extinct, which paved the way for Darwin's theory of evolution. More recently, Mary's place in the history of science has been recognised and books have been written about her. After a campaign by schoolgirl, Evie Swire, a statue of Mary and Tray was put up in Lyme Regis and unveiled on the anniversary of her 222$^{nd}$ birthday. You can visit the statue on the Gun Cliff Walk and go fossil hunting on the beach.

EmpathyLab

ZEPHYR

## We are an Empathy Builder Publisher

- Empathy is our ability to understand and share someone else's feelings
- It builds stronger, kinder communities
- It's a crucial life skill that can be learned

We are supporting **EmpathyLab** in their work to develop a book-based empathy movement in a drive to reach one million children a year and more.

Find out more at www.empathylab.uk
www.empathylab.uk/what-is-empathy-day

Zephyr is an imprint of Head of Zeus.
At Zephyr we are proud to publish books
you can read and re-read time and time
again because they tell a brilliant story
and because they entertain you.

@_ZephyrBooks

@_zephyrbooks

HeadofZeusBooks

readzephyr.com

www.headofzeus.com

ZEPHYR